I Am
Bill Gates'
Dog

I Am
Bill Gates'
DOG

JEFFREY ZYGMONT

I Am Bill Gates' Dog

Copyright © 2011 by Jeffrey Zygmont

ISBN: 978-0-9838131-0-1 (Paperback)
ISBN: 978-0-9838131-1-8 (eBook)
LCCN: 2011911870

Free People Publishing

Text layout and design by
Nancy Grossman
Back Channel Press
www.backchannelpres.com

Cover design by Paul Weston

Printed in the United States of America

for
Casey and Phyllis Zygmont
Requiescat in Pace

Acknowledgments

In gratitude.

Casey and Phyllis Zygmont, my parents, died on January 20 and November 12, 2009. By that time I had finished writing **I Am Bill Gates' Dog**, and I was investigating how to publish it and present it to you. My mother and father played no direct role in the book's creation or subsequent handling. But I have to acknowledge and express all of my thanks for their overarching influence and, especially, for the contributions they made to my formation.

Similarly, my own close family – my wife Donna, our children, their spouses and children – provide the inspiration, support and sustenance that I translate to literary endeavors. Although their contributions are indirect, they are so large that I must express gratitude.

More directly, graphic artist Paul Weston created the cover that draws you to this book. Paul maintains a virtual presence at www.instigatordesign.com.

Web designer Hyung Park built and maintains the web site that introduced many of you to **I Am Bill Gates' Dog**, and to my other books and poems. Hyung's signboard hangs at www.viamodern.com.

Randy Ross provided more encouragement and advice than I can reasonably expect from a friend and fellow author. Generously he continues to share the insights he acquires through his own determined efforts in literary marketing, promotion and all related activities an author must pursue to give his book a public life. Randy entertains visitors at www.RandyRoss-Media.com.

Finally, John and Nancy Grossman of Back Channel Press applied their publishing skills, and especially their expertise in self-publishing, to bring this book to you in an attractive and appealing format – including both the printed and e-book versions. They make www.backchannelpress.com a good destination for any writer exploring options in publishing.

CHAPTER 1

Inside the round conference room three advisors waited while Bill and Melinda, husband and wife, debated.

"I thought it was a stupid idea in the first place," said Bill Gates. "Now you're telling me I should have more dogs?"

"Not really," Melinda said. "Not more image dogs. This is something different. These other dogs will be for me. They're breeding dogs. If you want an image dog you can still have just one."

"I thought even one was stupid," Gates said. "We don't have time to be taking care of dogs around here. I don't care what they're for. Look what happened to the last one. It was a disaster. It was a complete disaster. The dog wouldn't do anything. What kind of an image is that?"

The three advisors sharing the table with Bill and Melinda waited longer. Franklin Osborne, the image consultant to Bill Gates, watched Melinda. He felt uncertain about how to react and he waited to see how Melinda would handle her husband's stubborn insistence. Cassie Welch, the image consultant to Melinda Gates, sat anxiously near the edge of her chair, eager for an opportunity. Reginald Macklam, the canine advisor, rested his head in his hand and stared down at a pad on the table, resisting an urge to doodle.

"I know it was a disaster," Melinda said to Bill while the three advisors waited. "I could see that as plain as day. That's the problem: the dogs aren't so smart anymore. It's the breeders' fault – all those damn puppy mills. All they pay attention to is how the dogs look. They don't pay any attention to their personalities or their intelligence or anything other than how they look."

"The damn thing didn't even follow me into the room," Gates said. "I had to go back and get it. It was nothing but a big disruption. How could anyone believe that it's my dog when it wouldn't even follow me into the room?"

Reginald Macklam looked up from his pad. "It just needed more training," he said.

"But you already trained it," shot Gates. "You said it was ready. I think it was just stupid." He turned to his wife. "Why the hell do you want to breed those dogs? They're stupid."

"That's exactly the problem," she answered. "They shouldn't be stupid. When I was a kid my Molly was the brightest dog I've ever seen. She was smart and she was affectionate too. But now the breed is losing all that. Now that they're popular, all the breeders want are the cute, fuzzy puppies that sell the easiest at the pet stores. They just take the best looking dogs. They don't take the best behaved dogs. Or the smartest dogs. They don't pay any attention to that. They just take the cutest ones and that poisons the gene pool. So with each generation, Aussies just get dumber and dumber. I hate that. I want it to stop."

"I just underestimated his loyalty," said Macklam, the canine expert. "He didn't follow you into the room, he stayed back with me because I was his master. At least in his eyes I was his master. That proved to be stronger than all the training we did. I should have known."

"We can't have any more mistakes like that," Bill Gates declared.

"The breeding dogs will be separate," said Melinda Gates. "They won't have to follow you anywhere."

Cassie Welch, the image consultant to Melinda Gates who sat at the edge of her chair, cut in: "You can almost see it as philanthropic, too, taking care of these dogs. It's certainly humanizing. It's diversifying, too. I mean, it's totally different from business and from your charity and from anything else that gets you in the news. Breeding dogs makes you look like a whole person. A caring person too. Those are all good things. They're all good for your image."

Cassie Welch and Franklin Osborne were image consultants with the agency Preen and Gloss. They had been hired by Bill Gates, and Melinda too, to change popular opinion. Even after Bill Gates had created the Bill and Melinda Gates Foundation – putting so many billions of his billions and billions of dollars into the trust to use for charity and good works – Gates had found that a lot of people still didn't like him. Most people still knew him only as "the world's richest man." A lot of people still resented the rough and tough business tactics he once had used to make his company, the Microsoft Corporation, so successful. Franklin Osborne and Cassie Welch, with the whole Preen and Gloss agency behind them, were hired to make publicity that would make people feel good about Bill Gates. Melinda, too.

The image-dog program aimed to make Bill Gates appear more like a common guy, like an ordinary Joe that other ordinary Janes and Joes could feel close to. He'd look like a nice guy if he had a pet dog. So an Australian shepherd was trained by Reginald Macklam to follow Gates devotedly when the Microsoft chairman attended meetings, addressed audiences, issued statements – whenever he showed himself in public. But the image dog had refused to follow Bill Gates into a meeting at the canine's first appearance last week.

"If you want to breed dogs on your own we don't need to talk about it now," said Gates to his wife. "Right now we have to get though this meeting agenda. Let's get on to the next item. If you want to breed dogs in private we can take it up later."

"But there's still the issue of the image dog," ventured Franklin Osborne, the image consultant assigned to Bill Gates. "That part's an agenda item and we haven't really dispensed with that."

"I thought it was a stupid idea when you brought it up the first time," Gates said to him.

"But it was a solution to a specific problem," the image man replied. "I mean, we all know how you feel about dogs and that's fine. But at the time we were casting around for a way to make you appear more casual and more commonplace and every-day. More like a regular guy. More, more . . .."

"More insouciant," cut in Cassie Welch, the image consultant assigned to Melinda Gates.

"Right," said Bill's image man. "More insouciant. We still have that need. I mean, even if this thing with the dog didn't work out last week, the original problem is still there. If a dog's not the answer, we might want to come up with another solution."

"Or we could try another dog," said Melinda. "Maybe an Aussie just wasn't the way to go. I'll take the fall for that one. I just love the breed so much that when we started talking about getting a dog, in my mind it just had to be an Australian Shepherd. Like my Molly when I was a girl. But maybe an Aussie just wasn't the way to go."

"I'll admit that when I first came up with the idea I was thinking more of just an ordinary, everyday dog," explained Osborne. "Not a fancy dog but, you know, a mutt, a common dog, something you'd get at, I don't know, the

SPCA animal shelter or something. Australian shepherds are fine. I mean, I didn't have anything against that, but I was picturing more of a plain ol' mutt that would be Bill's dog."

"Yeah," broke in Melinda's consultant Cassie Welch. "And when you think about it, an ordinary mutt fits really well with what we were trying to do in the first place. I mean, the whole reason for doing a dog and not something else is because of the link between dogs and the whole computer business and the software business, with the entrepreneurial spirit and the whole tech industry. You know, the freewheeling start-up company that doesn't have a lot of stodgy rules. The companies that guys start in their garages and end up making millions. Billions. Guys who don't even wear shoes at work. They let their employees bring their dogs to work. There's dogs laying down in the cubicles and walking over to the coffee machine and everything. Playing frisbee. That's the idea we wanted to get across: That Bill is a part of all that. He started Microsoft from nothing. Maybe it wasn't in a garage but it was like that. But now the only thing people think of is this enormous company as it exists today. The only thing people see is, quote, 'the world's richest man.' There's nothing about an entrepreneur. A dog is a great tie-in to that because it's part of the legend of the entrepreneur. Like the garage and the no-shoes and the pizza boxes and everything. Steve Jobs and Wozniak and all that. Just having a dog around ties into all that. And when you think about it, a plain ol', common dog fits the image even better."

"That was my original idea," concurred Osborne.

"So now you're saying I should have a sloppy dog follow me around," said Gates.

"A mongrel wouldn't be any sloppier than any other dog," Reginald Macklam responded. "It wouldn't be sloppier than an Aussie. It just wouldn't be pedigree. It wouldn't have breeding."

"You have to remember the original problem," said Bill's image handler Osborne. "We all know that creating your foundation was fantastic. Setting up the Bill and Melinda Gates Foundation to give so much of your money to just the right causes has already done so much. It's turned around your image completely. You're now a philanthropist and that's great. But stopping AIDS and stopping malaria is still pretty lofty stuff. It's great and it's ennobling and all that but it's still pretty remote for the average Joe. It's turned you into a nice guy. A caring guy. But it still doesn't make you real. Not to the average Joe. It still doesn't make you an ordinary guy that he can identify with. That's the goal. If ordinary people identify with you, they'll start to see you as a regular guy who made it big. Then you'll become a hero, instead of just a rich guy who keeps getting richer – a rich guy with so much money he gives it away to these causes. That's what you wanted, remember? You wanted the image of an ordinary guy who started with nothing. That way people will respect you and think you're a hero. That's why I was thinking of this whole entrepreneur idea of a guy who started with nothing. That's why we came up with the dog. In the public eye it ties into the image of a freewheeling entrepreneur. It's not enough all by itself, but it's a start. We'll have to do more of course to build that image. We figured the dog would be one little part, but little parts added together create a more convincing image than one big stunt."

"I still like the way it all fits together," said Cassie Welch. "Maybe the dog didn't work out last week, but at least now we know what *not* to do. And who knows, if Melinda ends up breeding Aussies, maybe it will make it easier for a new image dog because you can keep them all together. You know, keep a bunch of dogs instead of just one. Keep the breeding dogs and the image dog all together."

"Well, you wouldn't keep them together," said Reginald Macklam. "Not physically, I mean. You could keep them in the same kennel compound, but if you want to selectively breed them you have to keep the females isolated from the males, of course. You can't let the females and the males mix until you've selected the ones you want to mate, so there's no, you know, no accidents ahead of time."

"I don't see how you can change their personality," groused Bill Gates.

"Well, you do it the same as you selectively breed for any other characteristic," Macklam explained. "As you know, my background is in Hollywood. For the movies, I always wanted dogs that looked good and could act. Now, a dog can't act the way a person does. I mean, a dog can't pretend to be someone different, like a person actor does. So for dogs I looked for trainability, so they could obey commands on camera. I also paid a lot of attention to appearance, too, of course. But it's the same if you're breeding for other characteristics. You get a group of males and a group of females and you find the two that are closest to what you're looking for. You put those two together when the female goes into heat."

"So now we're supposed to have big groups of dogs around here," Gates grumbled.

"Maybe not groups," said Melinda. "Maybe just one group of male Aussies that we can choose from. For the females I think just one dog would be enough. Would that be okay, Reginald?"

"We could do it however you like," he answered. "The larger the pool, the better, but that obviously requires more work. If you want to keep it to a minimum, I'd say no fewer than four male dogs to choose from. We could watch their behavior and then choose the one that's closest to what you want."

"We're off the meeting agenda again," said Gates. "If these breeding dogs don't have anything to do with image dogs we shouldn't be talking about them."

"We were talking about image dogs," snipped his wife. "The breeding dogs are kind of in the same discussion. Especially if we're going to keep them together. I mean, in the same kennel compound, like Reginald said. I think it would help the image dog if he had other dogs around. Maybe one of our problems with Gandhi last week was that we had only one dog. He didn't have any companionship. An image dog might be happier if he lived with other dogs. Companionship is supposed to improve a dog's disposition, isn't that right, Reginald?"

"Well, yes, a lot of people think that," the trainer replied. "But remember, if you're serious about breeding you have to keep the groups somewhat isolated. If you want a mutt for an image dog I'd keep it in a separate enclosure. If you want it to have a companion, I'd just pick up another mongrel to stay in the same pen with it. I'd recommend a spayed female. A mature spayed female. They're a dime a dozen at the shelters."

"Now you're saying I'd need to have two image dogs," shot Gates.

"Well, no, not really," Macklam replied. "The companion would always stay in the kennel. You wouldn't ever have to even see it."

"And that's supposed to make this whole image-dog idea work out, after the big fiasco we had last week?"

"Well, that alone won't make a big difference, no," said Macklam. "We'd need to do some other things differently too. I think the dog would need to spend more time with you. You know: instead of just bringing it out when you're walking through the offices or when you're making some sort of media appearance or whatever it happens to be, we could keep the dog around you a little more during off times, you know, private times, just so it gets more used to you."

"What? Now you're saying I should have it around me like a real pet?"

After a moment of quiet, Cassie Welch broke in: "you have to admit, the whole thing fits together pretty nicely – the informal entrepreneur who made it big. But he's still a nice guy who just patters around with his dog."

"That's the image you want to make for yourself," said Osborne.

CHAPTER 2

Three dogs circled nose-to-anus like a carousel, each sniffing with intensity to fix identities onto the others. A fourth dog hung back, watching them warily from a near remove. It stretched toward them tentatively and pulled in air to probe their distant scents.

"Why don't you come over here," called one of the three carousel sniffers, a ginger-coated youth named Georgie.

"You guys are gonna catch something," the stand-alone dog replied.

"Catch something? Here?" gaped Georgie. "Look at this place. It's the cleanest place I've ever seen."

Blake, another of the three sniffers, lifted his head from Georgie's anus to peer around.

"It's nice all right," Blake said.

"It's the nicest place I've ever seen," repeated Georgie. "Look at this fence. It's shiny. I think it's even been washed."

The stand-alone dog pulled farther away from the group. He pattered cautiously toward the fence, approaching it slowly with his head low. He glanced once more at the three sniffing dogs before cautiously he stretched from his shoulders to sniff the bottom run of chain link.

"Everything's new," said Georgie with the group of three. "The cement here is clean. I don't think anyone's even walked on it before."

"It's nice to be first," said Blake. "And it's about time, too."

"I hope I stay here forever," said Georgie. He spun suddenly around and faced the third sniffing dog, which had gone for Georgie's anus. "Knock it off now," Georgie snarled. "Can't you see we're done with all that? You should have enough by now anyway."

"Okay, I got enough," said the chastened dog. He was a tall, tan Aussie named Web. "I'm done now too," Web said.

"Hey," called Dremmel, the dog at the fence who hung back from the others. "You guys ought to come over here and check this out. Over here by the fence. Down at this end. Smell this here. We're not the first ones. Someone else was here before. Not very long before, either. I thought I smelled something earlier but now I'm sure of it. Over here by the fence. There's not much here but there's definitely enough for me to say that somebody was here before. Just a little while ago, too. It's funny there's not more, but there's enough for me to say he was here. He was definitely here."

"Who was he," asked Web.

"I don't know," answered Dremmel, the hang-back dog. "You never know. You smell other guys all over the place but you never see 'em. You never know who they are."

"Yeah," said Georgie. "I smell what you're saying. There used to be somebody here all right. But who cares? Even if we're not the first ones, we're almost the first ones. Besides, look at this place. Even if there was a hundred others living here before us, this would still be the best place in the world. I want to stay here forever."

"I'm gonna stay," said Blake.

"But what about this other guy," asked Dremmel. "Don't you think he wanted to stay here, too? Where is he? He's gone and there's barely a trace of him here and nobody knows anything about him. We don't know who he was or when he was here or where he went to. Don't you ever wonder about that? It's the same thing everyplace else you go. There was always all sorts of other people there doing all sorts of other things, but then they're just gone. They're gone just like that and nobody ever knows where."

"I never thought about that before," said Web. "Where do you think everybody goes?"

"Why don't you go ask 'em," Georgie sneered. He laughed.

"I wouldn't laugh if I was you," warned Dremmel. "You might be next, you know. That's what scares me. There's always all these other guys and they're always just gone. Gone. Gone to who knows where. I don't want that to happen to me."

"Who says it's gonna happen to you," flipped Georgie.

"You just have to obey all the commands," said Blake. "You'll be safe if you obey all the commands. Heck, I was born to do that. I can do everything I'm told to do."

"Me too," echoed Web.

"What about this guy who was here before us?" Dremmel challenged. "This guy who's gone now? Maybe he followed all the commands."

"But you have to do it perfectly," answered Blake.

"Hey," Georgie interrupted, "you guys oughtta knock it off and take a look at this."

"What," asked Web.

"Look who's coming," said Georgie. "Look at that girl. D'yuh think she's coming in here?"

"She's going to the other side," Blake said. "It looks like she's going to be over on the other side."

"Yeah, but she's still right here," Georgie said. "There's just this fence between us and then she's right here."

The four dogs watched as a young Australian shepherd walked with the kennel keeper into their compound. The dog stepped daintily with the discernible pride of breeding. A lustrous red merle coat of cinnamon flecks on silver napping flounced from her withers to her tail. As she drew closer the four dogs could see that her eyes were crystal blue. The kennel keeper settled the young female in a pen inside the building that connected to the four long runs outside that were separated by chain link fencing. Standing four abreast at the fence, the stricken males watched the new lady through a broad window that let daylight flood into the kennel house. Maybe eleven months old, the graceful belle sat politely while the kennel keeper scooped food from a high bin into a wide stainless dish. She ran fresh water into another.

"You be sure to drink a lot after your trip," the keeper said to the girl dog. "I gave you some food here too, if you want it. This here is your house and you can go out the back door there whenever you want to get to your yard. I'll leave you alone for a while to get used to the place, but first I better go say hello to those hooligans out there."

The kennel keeper stepped lightly out of the building, entering the girl-dog's run and walking along the fence to where the four males watched from the other side.

"Hi, guys," she called as she approached. "You guy's getting used to the place?" She bent to regard them through the fence. "I brought a new friend for you. Her name is Amanda. She's here just for you. Or maybe it's the other way around: I guess you're here just for her. One of you is, anyway. One of you guys gets to mate with her. That's the whole reason you're here: to make more of you." The kennel keeper fished into a pocket for four small biscuits.

"Here's one for each of you," she said. Georgie snapped fast to grab the first biscuit she passed through the fence. Blake took the next, followed by

Web.

"Here's one for you too," the keeper said to Dremmel, who approached her more cautiously.

"You're a bunch of good guys," she said to the group. "I'd keep all of you guys if I could. I'd of kept big Gandhi, too. He was the smartest dog I've seen in a while. So loyal and loving besides. Reggie said Bill Gates didn't like him. That's why he had to go. I say too bad for Bill Gates. Too bad that it's not up to me. If I was in charge he'd still be around. But don't worry. At least one of you guys will get in here with Amanda. That's the whole reason you're here: to get one of you in here so you can make more of you. First we just gotta figure out who."

As the kennel keeper stepped lightly away through Amanda's enclosure, she twisted once to glance backward at them and wave. Georgie stood full forward and pressed his nose to the fence as he peered after her. He stared inside the room where the girl dog ate slowly with poise from the wide stainless bowl.

"We get to marry her," breathed Georgie.

"No, only one of us does," Dremmel corrected.

"It better be me," Georgie said.

Blake interjected: "I can already do everything right."

"We all can," said Dremmel.

"I do it perfectly," Blake insisted.

"Look at her place," said Web. "Her place is bigger than ours. And it has that tree on the end and all that cool gravel underneath it. I love to lay down in gravel. How come her place is so much bigger than ours?"

"'Cause she's the lady," answered Georgie. "Besides, it won't be her place much longer. Didn't you hear that one of us gets to marry her?"

"But there's more of us in here," said Web. "Even after one of us goes in there, there'll still be more of us in here."

Georgie glanced all around their enclosure. "This will still be a real nice place to stay," he said. "This will still be a lot nicer than anyplace else you'll ever find."

"What makes you think you'll stay here," said Dremmel. "That's what I'm tryin' to say. Nobody stays around. Not for very long. Look what happened to that other one. Who did she say? Big Gandhi? He was the one here before us. Look what happened to Big Gandhi. He's gone and you hardly can tell he was ever around."

"Who's Bill Gates," wondered Blake.

"He's the one who didn't like Big Gandhi," Dremmel said. "Didn't you hear her? He's the whole reason Big Gandhi is gone. Who knows where he went. All we know is that he's not here now and what makes you think that won't happen to you? Maybe one of us will marry her and we'll get to have babies but what about the rest of us? We'll be just like Big Gandhi. I know it."

"You mean we have to be the one who gets to marry her if we want to stay around?" asked Web.

"That's the only way," warned Dremmel.

"You don't know that," challenged Georgie.

"Then what about Big Gandhi?" Dremmel retorted. "Why isn't Big Gandhi still here anymore?"

"He's gone 'cause Bill Gates didn't like him," Georgie argued.

"We all heard the keeper say that we're here to make more. We all heard her say that's the only reason we're here," Dremmel said.

"That's not a bad reason," said Georgie. He pressed his nose to the fence once again. "I mean, look at her. Look at her eating in there. I never seen a lady so beautiful. An' take it from me: I looked. I looked at 'em all. I never seen any that look just like her. Even if this wasn't the best place going"

– he gazed carefully all around the kennel compound, apprising the enclosure he shared and then peering through the fence at the fenced yards beyond his – "even if this wasn't the best place around, it would still be incredible to get in there with her. But this *is* the best place. The best place with the most beautiful lady."

"The best with the best," Blake repeated. "I always knew this was coming. I was made for this."

"But only one of us gets it," warned Dremmel.

Web said, "I wonder which one it will be."

CHAPTER 3

The dog pens inside the kennel building were spacious rooms that were tiled on the floor and tiled on the walls. But the walls inside the kennel's small office remained unpainted. Chalky plaster striped the seams and smeared the screw dents that dotted the drab wallboard surrounding Reginald Macklam and the kennel keeper, Debbie Green, as they sat inside the small office. The room smelled of gypsum. Macklam and Green sat with their knees pushed uncomfortably against a gray metal desk. They stared for a moment unmoving at a laptop computer opened vacantly upon the desk. At last Debbie Green said, "I can't do this."

"What do you mean you can't do it?" asked Macklam.

"I hate these things," she said. "That's why I quit my last job. They started me on a computer and I just didn't want to do it."

"But it's easy," said Macklam.

"I hate it," she said.

"How can you hate it? It's part of a job."

"I just hate sitting down here and moving that little arrow around. I hate typing. It takes so long. I'd rather be out doing things. I'd rather be out with the dogs. I like animals."

"But this won't take long," said Macklam. "It's just some questions. It's just a report so she can figure out which dog she likes the best. You only have to do it once a day."

"Why can't you do it and I'll just keep looking after the dogs?"

"I am doing it," he answered. "I have to do it and you have to do it. She wants to get one from both of us, to help her decide. It's just an attribute list. It's just some questions. It won't take you long."

"But I don't like the questions," said Debbie Green. "And why does there have to be so many of them?"

"Well, I wondered a little bit about that myself. I mean, I thought the form was kind of picky, too. I don't think she needs to know all of this. I mean, if you get into too much detail it can just make the job all the harder – I mean, make it harder for her to decide rather than easier. But she's the employer, and this is how she wants it."

"When you hired me I thought it was just to take care of the dogs. You didn't say anything about this."

"That's because this is something new," Macklam responded. "The job is different now. When we started there was just going to be one dog. Just one dog and the only thing he had to do was pretend he liked Bill Gates. You remember Gandhi. But now we have seven. Or we're going to have seven very soon. That's why we expanded this place, remember? That's why you had the last four weeks off: so we could make room for all these dogs. We talked about all this. You said you'd love to have more dogs and you were excited about it. That's why you waited the four weeks even though they wouldn't let me pay you for them."

"I was excited about the dogs," said Green. "You never said anything about computers. I hate these things."

"Look," replied Macklam, "the whole reason you have five Aussies out there is because the missus suddenly got a thing for those dogs and now she wants to breed them. She wants to make super dogs and that's why those four boys are out there: so she can pick the one she likes best. That's what this form is for. It's just an attribute evaluation form. She wants to know which dog has the behavior she likes best. You have to do one every day and I have to do one every day. But it's a lot easier doing them on a computer than it is by hand. Believe me, I'm from the day when we had to write them out. This is a lot easier."

"Not for me. I hate those things. You never said anything about having to use a computer."

"Well you might have figured it out," shot Macklam. "These are computer people, after all. They own the world's biggest computer company. It's not a stretch to think that, working for them, you'll use a computer somewhere or other."

"I quit my last job because they wanted me to start using a computer," she sniffed.

"But you have to use a computer on any job you can find out there."

"I just want to work with the dogs. That's why I took this job. I want to work with, you know, with living things. With animals."

"All right," said Macklam, "we'll do it this way: I'll print a whole bunch out for you. I'll give you a stack of them. You can do them by hand and then give them to me and I'll type them into the computer for you. But you have to do it every day. You can't skip a day and you can't be late. It's a damn picky list and if I'm going to do this I don't want to be waiting around for them."

"You mean I can do them with a pencil?"

"Pencil or pen, I don't care. I'm just going to throw them away when I'm done. They have to be in the computer because that's the only way the missus is going to look at them. They have this fancy program that will tabulate all the results and rate the dogs based on our answers. I think the computer will end up picking the dog. That's the way I think it will work out, no matter what they say now. But they can't have the computer do anything if you're writing them by hand."

"I'm sorry to be so much trouble," she said more brightly.

"Just don't tell them we're doing this," said Macklam. "And don't let them see you filling them out. It'll be better if they don't know about this. Just let them think you're doing them all by yourself on the computer."

"I will."

"And don't leave them lying around. The blank forms, I mean. Hide them deep in a drawer in here and don't leave them out."

"I won't."

"Now listen," said Macklam, "here's the other thing we need to go over. The other two dogs, they're ready now so you can head over and pick them up. They're expecting you this afternoon at the shelter. I had our vet check them out and they're just as I thought: two fit and healthy mongrels with no kinds of serious defects. They're mutts but they're good looking dogs. I think they'll be perfect."

"And I'm supposed to keep them together?"

"That's right. I tried them out together and I think they'll do fine. The second one is a nine-year-old female. Her name is Ester. She's a docile dog. Very friendly. They wanted her just for companionship and socialization for the male. He's two years old. A strong, playful guy. He's a happy dog. I think he'll do just perfectly."

"But he's a mix?"

"That's right. At the shelter they said he's a shepherd-lab cross. But they say that about every dog they get. Every large dog, anyway. They don't know the parentage, of course. Like I said before, these are just strays that the police pick up, or that somebody just drops off without a word. They're unwanted. But they're damn nice dogs."

"Should I put them in the third run, next to Amanda?"

"No," Macklam said. "Put them over in the fourth. We'll keep the third run open as the spare. There's no reason to put them right next to the Aussies. They have each other for company. That's why we're getting the second dog anyway. That's why we're getting Ester. She'll be together with Rin so there's no reason to keep them so close to the breeding dogs. We'll keep the two groups far apart."

"Rin is the name of the boy dog?" asked kennel keeper Debbie Green.

"That's right. That's what they were calling him at the pound and I see no reason to change it. He'll be Bill Gates' dog."

"So we have to go through all that again."

"Well, we plan to do things differently this time."

"If Bill Gates didn't like Gandhi I don't see how he'll like this new dog," said Green. "I thought Gandhi was a real good dog."

"I thought he was an exceptional dog," said Macklam.

"I hated to see him go," said Green. "I still worry about him a lot."

"Well, we'll try to do better this time. I think Bill Gates will try harder this time, too. He doesn't give a damn about dogs. In fact, I think he positively dislikes them. But he's awfully worried about history. Tomorrow's history, I mean. He's afraid of the reputation he's earned and he's afraid that's how he's going to be remembered forever after. They've hired all these high-flying image consultants to try to change people's minds. They're all convinced that having a dog will do that – help do that, anyway. People will think he's a nice guy if he goes around with a dog all the time. They'll think he's an average guy just like old Clem down the street. Our job is to make it look like he really owns the dog. We're supposed to make it look like Rin is really his dog."

"But I don't see how just having a dog can make him look nice," said Green.

"Well, it's not *just* the dog. I mean, they're doing other things too," Macklam explained. "The dog is just a part of this whole big campaign they started to make him look like he's a nice little fellow who just happened to become the world's richest man. There's other parts, too. Hell, they've been running the biggest part for some time now, ever since they started the Bill and Melinda Gates Foundation and dumped a load of their money into it. You've heard about that, I'm sure."

"No," said Green, "I don't think I ever heard of it."

"It's just a charity they started," Macklam explained. "They paid for it and they control it and now it gives them their ticket to jet all over the world and talk at all of these big conferences. You know: conferences about saving the world. They talk about healing the sick and raising the dead and all that."

"I guess maybe I have heard about that," said Green. "Bill Gates is very generous."

"He pays a lot of money to make you think that," Macklam quipped.

"Pays it to who?"

"To his charity, of course."

CHAPTER 4

The four boy dogs lived in the first of four spacious pens inside the kennel building. Amanda stayed in the second one, abutting the boys' home. The pens exited to outdoor runs. The four runs stood side-by-side in a row, creating adjacent outdoor play areas separated by chainlink fencing. Amanda's run, the second in the line, enclosed a shade-casting tree at its end, neatly bottomed by gravel.

Inside the building, the pen that was shared by the four guys – the first pen in the line of four – was divided by partition walls into four individual rooms for the fellows. Kennel keeper Debbie Green had just set out four bowls of food and had run fresh water for the four boys. Georgie gulped down his bowlful of kibble in snaps. He scurried out of his partitioned room before even lapping some water. He turned into Web's room and nosed into the food bowl while Web still ate. Silently, without lifting his head, Web stepped and maneuvered his body to push Georgie away from his meal. Georgie relented. He stepped back, and then stuck his nose into Web's water bowl. While he drank he caught sight through the open doorway of Amanda outside in the neighboring run, venturing into her yard for the first time since her arrival. Georgie dashed quickly outside to greet her.

"Hi," he beamed at her.

"Hi," said Amanda.

"My name is Georgie. I live in here with those three other guys. They're all inside eating though."

"Aren't you hungry too?" asked Amanda.

"Nah. I'm all right," Georgie answered. "Hey, there's more to life than a bowlful of food, you know."

Amanda grinned.

"It's pretty nice out here, isn't it?" asked Georgie.

"It's very nice," she agreed.

"It's the nicest place I've ever seen," Georgie said. "Everything's new and it's all washed up and everything. It's so big. I like it here a lot."

They stood on their separate sides of the fence, gazing with admiration all around the compound.

"Hey," said Georgie, "did you hear about Bill Gates?"

"Who's Bill Gates," she asked.

"He's the boss. I guess that's what you'd call him. He's in charge of everything. He's the one who tells everybody what to do."

"Even Debbie Green?"

"Yep, he even tells the kennel keeper what to do. He's in charge of everything. He's the one who didn't like Big Gandhi."

"Who's Big Gandhi?" Amanda asked.

"Big Gandhi is the one who was here before us. He's the one who's gone now. Come over here and smell the fence real carefully."

As Amanda stepped and stretched and gingerly put her nose to the fence, Georgie gazed at her with sybaritic delight.

"Oh yeah," she said. "I didn't notice him before. This is my first time out here."

"That's okay," said Georgie. "He's hard to notice because everything's been washed so clean. But that's Big Gandhi for sure. I never met him. Nobody did. And now he's just gone. Did you ever notice that? Did you ever notice how everyplace you go there's been all sorts of other people there before you but then they're just gone with no trace and you never know anything about them? You never know where they've gone? I notice that all the time."

"That sounds very deep," said Amanda with admiration.

"I know. I think about stuff like that all the time. But not too much. I just wonder about things a lot. Things you can't understand."

"Like Big Gandhi?"

"Yeah, like Big Gandhi. He was a great guy. A really great guy. But Bill Gates didn't like him so now he's gone."

"Bill Gates can do that?"

"Oh, yeah. Bill Gates can do anything."

Web trotted out of the kennel building to join Amanda and Georgie. His greater height appeared almost awkward as he stood shoulder to shoulder beside the other male.

"This is Web," Georgie said to Amanda. "He lives in here too."

"Hi, Web," she chirped. "My name is Amanda. Oh, I'm sorry, Georgie. I never told you my name."

"That's okay," said Georgie. "I already know you're Amanda. I mean, Debbie Green told us that when she brought you in here."

"Debbie Green tells us everything," said Web.

"There's two other guys, too," Georgie explained. "But they're still inside."

"There's four of us in here, but your side is bigger than ours," said Web.

"I don't mind," said Georgie. "I think you should have the biggest side. Besides, in a little while you're gonna marry one of us. There'll be two of us in there then. That will even things off a little."

"Marry?" said Amanda.

"Yeah. Didn't Debbie tell you? That's the whole reason we're here. One of us will marry you so we can have babies. And, hey, once the babies come we'll need all that room in there."

"Babies!" Amanda said.

"Yeah. I can't wait to have a whole bunch of babies," said Georgie. "I already know what I'm gonna name 'em."

"I'm gonna name one of mine Web," Web said.

Georgie laughed mockingly. "Web wants his kids to be just like him," he cut.

"I do," said Web.

"Ha," Georgie chided.

"That's sweet," said Amanda.

"But they want all the babies to be smart," explained Georgie. "You get to marry the one of us that's smartest."

"Is that you?" she asked.

"Well, nobody can say anything definite yet," he answered. "I mean, officially nobody is supposed to say anything. But I think you can figure it out."

Web broke in: "Dremmel said Bill Gates gets to decide."

"Who's Dremmel?" asked Amanda.

"Oh, he's just one of the guys in the house," Georgie answered. "He's just a big spoiler. He's always saying you shouldn't do this and you shouldn't do that. He's afraid to do anything."

"Dremmel says that once you get married, the rest of us will be gone," said Web.

"Gone like Big Gandhi?" she asked him.

"Just like Big Gandhi," he answered. "Dremmel says the three of us that are left will just vanish and nobody will know anything about us."

"Hey, look," interrupted Georgie. "Who are those two people over there?"

Together Amanda, Georgie and Web gazed across the compound to the far pen, to the last fenced yard in the run of four. A pair of rangy, indeterminate hounds stood looking back at them. One was an older lady. The other was a dark-haired, eager young male. The two newcomers stood a little apart from each other, tentative, uncomfortable about getting too close.

"I don't know who they are," said Web. "I've never seen 'em before."

"They haven't been here before," said Georgie. "Look at 'em. They're just checkin' the place out. They're lookin' around like they've never seen a place like this before."

"Like me," said Amanda.

"They're nothin' like you," replied Georgie. "Look at 'em. They're way too scroungie to be anything like you. They're mixed breeds."

"I mean they're new just like me," she explained.

"They don't know what they're doing," Georgie said.

"Hey, you guys," Web called to them. "What are you guys doing over there?"

"Shut up," hissed Georgie. "What are you calling over there for? We don't want to talk to them and we sure don't want them to talk to us."

"I just wondered who they are," said Web.

"We just got here," the young male in the far enclosure called back. "We just came out now to have a look around."

"Don't say anything back," Georgie commanded in a hushed tone. "Whatever we do, we don't want to start talking to them."

"But I already asked them," said Web.

The young man called over again: "Have you people been here for long?"

"Don't answer," Georgie repeated.

"My name is Rin," the newcomer told them. "And this here is Ester."

"Don't say a thing," Georgie warned Web and Amanda.

"But isn't that kind of rude," said Amanda. "I mean, we asked them first. And they're both just right over there."

"It's not rude. They're two whole fences away," Georgie said. "There's that whole open yard between your place and theirs."

"I just wondered who they are," said Web.

"Who cares? They're way over there. And look at 'em. They're nothing like us. They're mixed. They're non-breeds. You can see that just by looking at 'em. They don't have the breeding we have."

"I just feel kind of funny not saying anything to them," Amanda said.

"That's the last thing we want to do. We don't want to say anything to them. If we start talking to them now, they'll think they can do it all the time. That's the last thing we want. We don't want them coming out here and talking to us all the time. They'll think they're like us. Then they'll want to have all the things that we have."

"They could never be just like us," said Amanda.

"No kidding," said Georgie. "Just so long as they understand that. That's what I want to make sure of. I want to make sure that they don't get the wrong ideas. Let them stay over there where they belong. They can look over here if they want. But let 'em stay way over there. This here is for us. This here is the nicest place there could be."

"Maybe they're going to have babies too," Web wondered out loud. "That place over there will get real crowded if they have any babies."

"Let it," said Georgie. "It'll be their own fault."

"She can't have babies," said Amanda. "Look at how old she is."

"But he can," said Web.

"Of course he can," snapped Georgie. "Anyone can. But who'd want to have his babies. Let him stay way over there with that old dog. She can have him."

"Maybe she's his mother," Web wondered.

"She's not his mother," Georgie mocked. "How could she be his mother? She doesn't look anything like him."

"But with that kind they don't always look the same," Amanda put in. "I mean, kids don't always look like their mothers when they're non-breeds. Sometimes nonnies look pretty different from their parents."

"Maybe he'll come over here and we can ask him," Web said.

"He can't come here," Georgie shot out. "We can't let him ever come here. We can't let him get anywhere close to Amanda."

"But he looks okay," said Amanda. "He looks like he's a nice guy."

"No he doesn't. And who cares what he looks like anyway. He doesn't look like one of us. That's 'cause he isn't one of us. He isn't anything like us. He doesn't have breeding. This side over here, this side with Amanda's tree and everything, this side is just for us. It's real clean over here. Everything's brand new. If they come over here it won't be the same then. We'll have to share everything. It'll get crowded. They don't have breeding. We can't let 'em have this. That'll ruin everything. You want to keep all this, don't you?" he asked Amanda.

"Georgie is real smart," said Web. "He knows all about this kind of stuff."

CHAPTER 5

Reginald Macklam passed a pouch across the table to Bill Gates.

"The last time we tried this you didn't like keeping these in your pocket," Macklam explained. "When we tried it back with Gandhi, I mean. This time you can just keep them right here in this sack here. The important thing is that you give him one only when it's appropriate. As a reward when he does something right. That might make it easier now that you're going to be in a group of people with him for the first time. But give them sparingly. They're just to be used as a backup and I don't want you to overuse them. Some trainers use treats all the time, but that's only because it's so easy. I do things differently. Just remember to reward only the right behavior. And remember, the *right* behavior is whatever you want him to do. You're in charge of controlling his actions."

"What about when it does something wrong?" asked Gates.

"Just ignore him. Push him off or call him off if he's too intrusive, but for the most part you can just ignore him when he does something you don't want. Pretend he's not even there. If you praise him when he's good, reward him when he's good, and ignore him when he's bad, he'll catch on really quickly to what you want from him."

"So if he bites someone I should just ignore it?" panned Gates.

"He won't get that bad. I'm sure of that," Macklam said. "So far he's done very well with you. But so far it's been just the two of you alone together. It might be a little bit different this time because there's going to be other people with you in this meeting here. His behavior might be a little bit different this time, I mean, because the situation is different now. We'll see how he does. These biscuits might make a good distraction if he should need a distraction. Just don't overuse them. I'll say it again: I've never been too keen on the treats. They can make it too easy – make training too easy, I mean. He'll come to expect them all the time and then you won't get a legitimate bond between the two of you. But today they might help you a little. I can help you a little today too. I'll be right here in the background. I expect to stay in the background, but I can always step in if things should get too far out of line. And remember, his name is Rin. Call him by name and praise him when it's appropriate and he'll get the hang of things in a hurry."

Gates glanced up at the clock hung high on the wall.

"Let's just make sure he doesn't interrupt this meeting," he said.

"I don't expect that he will," replied Macklam. "I certainly hope that he doesn't. But of course, I can't absolutely guarantee that."

"I hope that he doesn't too," said Gates. "If this is going to work out at all, he can't get in the way of any important business. And this meeting right now is about very important business. I've got two big events to prepare for. Two important events. That's what this meeting is about today. We have to wrap up our planning for them. It's critical, and we have to get through it without any interference from ... from ... what's his name again?"

"Rin."

"Right. From Rin. I can't have him around if he's going to get in the way of business. When I agreed to try this again, it was under the condition that it wouldn't get in the way, that all the critical things that I have to do will still get done without any interruptions. If not, it's just not worth it and he's gone."

"Whether he's gone or whether he stays is your call, Bill. It's always been your call," said Macklam. "The way that I see it, you're paying me to see that it gets done right. But whether or not it's worth getting done – that decision is up to you."

"All right," said Gates as he glanced upward at the wall clock again. "So let's see how he does and I'll decide based on that. I need to get things started now. I'm not going to hold up the meeting for this."

"We still have about two minutes," Macklam said. "I'll have Debbie bring him in now and leave him here next to you. That will give him a moment or two to get settled before the others arrive. Remember, his name is Rin. Maybe give him a pat when Debbie brings him in here to you."

Rin stood with native dignity and upright self-assurance beside the chair where Bill Gates sat. Three people filed silently into the round conference room for the start of the meeting. Prepped in advance by Macklam, they disregarded Rin as they settled into seats. They hinged open notebook computers, brought out pads and clicked open pens without so much as a glance at the dog. Rin watched them, inquisitive and alert. He sat down tentatively on the floor beside the chairman's seat, his mien still probing and forward.

Around the table sat Franklin Osborne, the image consultant to Bill Gates, as well as Albert Wistol and Cynthia Boyd. Albert Wistol was a publicity reader. He had joined the Preen and Gloss image-building firm to work on the Bill and Melinda Gates program. Wistol went through newspaper and magazine articles, reviewed television news reports and other video clips, he scanned web postings and blogs and searched for every other fleeting mention or public discussion about Bill Gates. His was paid to report on what image and reputation Gates possessed with the public, and how that reputation improved, by reviewing how the whole wide-ranging media portrayed the software billionaire. Cynthia Boyd, sitting next to Wistol, was the private speech writer for Bill Gates.

Only Albert Wistol felt anxious about Rin. He felt immeasurably anxious. He ignored the dog, as Macklam had instructed them all to do in a memo before the meeting. But from the instant he entered the room – despite all the elaborate, secret preparations he had made, the silent, repetitive chants, the relaxation exercises and rhythmic breathing – he felt overwhelmed by the ancient, irrational terror. Once seated, he stared hard at the screen of the laptop computer he opened on the table in front of him, trying to focus all of his attention on something, anything, that was not Rin. Wistol worried that sweat would moisten his top lip and temples. He wanted to shrink and disappear. He wanted to become unseen, hidden and anonymous. He fretted that his primitive fear of canines would show too plainly with only four people present at the meeting – five if you counted Macklam discretely seated against the wall behind Bill Gates. Wistol viciously envied him. He wished he could swap roles with Macklam and become a stand-by observer instead of a meeting participant. Soon he would have to speak. He dreaded how his voice would let the others sense his plain fright so clearly. Rin would notice too, he worried. Wistol sat concertedly still, afraid that any small word or even a slight movement might alert the attention of the animal he dreaded.

"Okay," said Gates unaware. "This is the last big meeting we're going to have about both of these items, so we need to wrap everything up today. After today we'll just meet individually, as needed. But today is the last chance we have to discuss these things all together as a group. It's the same two things we've been talking about – two *big* things. First we have my Thinking Week up at the lodge. Then comes the Harvard commencement. They're our two best shots this summer, so we can't make any mistakes. We need to make sure that everything goes just right. I want them both to send exactly the right message."

"Right," said image-consultant Franklin Osborne. "We have to send exactly the right message. This is our big push now. This is when we have a chance to really make a difference, to really push that new image. We have to do it *now*. Right *now!*"

"The first one on our agenda is Thinking Week," said Gates.

"Right," said Osborne, elaborating officiously to Wistol and Boyd. "That's coming right up. That one's right on top of us and we're all set with it. We put it on the agenda today just in case there were any lingering issues we need to discuss. But it looks like we're all set. That one should go really well. That's our Thinking Week interview. Remember? It's next week. It will let us show that Bill is more than just a businessman. It will show that he's done more at Microsoft than just run the company and make all sorts of money. That's what Albert sees all too often in the media. Remember? This idea that Bill's not a tech guy but just a businessman. That's what we need to change. We need to make him look more like Steve Jobs and some of those other guys. You know: the entrepreneur and tech innovator who changed the world with computers and all these other new products. I-pods and everything. Jobs gets all the credit for that, while Bill is just, quote, 'the world's richest man.'"

"Jobs is the same age as me," Gates stated.

"He just got to the image before you did," said Osborne. "He's got that tech-guru image. That's the only thing he's got on you."

"The Thinking Week is all about technology," said Gates. "It's all about new ideas and nothing else. But it's got to send exactly that message."

"That's right," said Osborne. "And I think it will. The Thinking Week should go very well. I think we're all set up for that one. I mean, there's not a whole lot more we can say about it now. There's no speech or anything. It's just Bill's week alone up at Caveat Lodge, when he takes a stack of papers and reports written by Microsoft people about their new ideas. He reads through them all one by one and makes notes and decides what to do about them. It's intensely private. At least that's how we're billing it: Just Bill and all these research papers from Microsoft people and he's alone so he can think about their ideas. A thinking week. We have the reporter from the New York Times coming in just for one day. More like half a day, really. He's coming in just to observe. Just to see Bill thinking about all these new ideas from Microsoft people. We're giving him an exclusive so he's agreed to our terms – any reporter would for exclusive access to Bill Gates. He'll write an article about it for the Times, and that'll be great for showing how Bill is a leading technologist. You're a guy with ideas, not just, you know, the money and all that. But there's not a lot more to say about it. Not now, anyway. We're all set with the reporter. He'll be there for sure and it'll just be the two of you together, so we can control that one pretty easily," said Osborne.

"What about our friend over there?" asked Cynthia Boyd as she gestured toward Rin.

"Oh, yeah. The image dog might be there too," Osborne added. "He's done real well so far, so we're thinking about sending him to the lodge for the reporter to see with Bill. But only if he's ready. If he's ready, the Thinking Week will be the first time he'll be seen anywhere with Bill. So we might be getting started again with that whole, subtle, image-dog thing at Thinking Week, too."

"I think he's ready," said Boyd. "I definitely think he should go. Look at how nicely he's sitting right now."

She gazed playfully at Rin. Meanwhile, Albert Wistol kept his eyes locked on the laptop he had pulled up close to fill his field of vision. *This is fantastic,* he said to himself, relieved but still tremulous too. *This is absolutely amazing. We've gotten through one item. That has to be half of the meeting. And I haven't had to say a word. I haven't even had to move.*

"He's such a pretty guy," said Cindy Boyd as she looked at Rin.

"That brings us to Harvard," Osborne went on. "It's such a huge opportunity." He spread his hands wide across the table to emphasize the immensity of it. "We really gotta get working on that one. I mean, that one speech has the potential to be covered all over the place. It's a great human interest story. I mean, everybody knows you dropped out of Harvard, Bill. That's okay, because then you went on to start the world's biggest company. But now, what, about thirty years later, Harvard comes back and wants you to give its commencement address. It's the world's most prestigious university. Its graduation address is one of the most prestigious speeches anyone can give. You're its most famous drop-out. It's a perfect story."

"But only if I deliver just the right message," said Gates. "Maybe all those pieces fit together just fine on their own. But it's not enough for me just to give a speech there. I need a message with a lot of impact. Something that gets noticed. Something that gives people something to talk about. That shows what we stand for and shows that we're about more than just money."

"We just need to decide what we stand for," said Osborne.

"It has to have a high moral content," said Gates.

"That's right," said Osborne. "We can forget all about software. We can forget about business. For this we need to go right to the Foundation. We need to stick exclusively to that. You can talk about charity and giving. You can talk about philanthropy and the importance of giving back. And of course you can tie all of that into the Bill and Melinda Gates Foundation. You can tie it into your own philanthropy and talk about why you started the Foundation in the first place."

"But you've already done all that," interrupted Cindy Boyd, the speech writer. "I mean, if that's all you want, I can crank out a speech for you pretty easily. I can just knead together a lot of the other talks you've already given about the Foundation. About why you started it and how it ties into the importance of giving something back and all that. But I thought you wanted something different for Harvard. I thought you wanted something that says more than that."

"We never really decided on a topic," said Osborne. "That's why we scheduled this meeting here today."

Gates frowned. He pushed back against his chair. "But you're right," he said. "I need to go higher. I need to talk about something at a higher level. Something that's above the Foundation. Something more universal. Values and morals and all that."

"Of course," agreed Osborne. "But you can still use the Gates Foundation as an illustration to show those values and morals in action. I mean, it's a darn good illustration."

"But if you talk about the Foundation it's going to sound like you're talking about yourself," said Boyd. "It'll sound like, like…"

"Like propaganda," Gates finished.

"It might."

Gates rocked backward in his chair and pressed his fingertips together.

"Cindy is certainly right about one thing," said Osborne. "You've certainly talked about the Foundation a lot this year. We've raised a lot of awareness. That part of the program is going real well. It's been really successful."

Gates looked across the table at the publicity reader, Albert Wistol.

"Is that still growing?" he asked the specialist. "Is awareness of the Foundation still going up, or has it started to level off by now?"

Wistol glanced up at the chairman, but all he could see was Rin, the canine, seated beside Bill Gates. Wistol looked quickly back down at the notebook computer. He wiggled to pull it in closer against his body. He felt perspiration ooze from his pores.

"It's still growing," he said, close to blurting. "I mean, I think, oh, I had it here a second ago." Wistol fumbled with the laptop pointer and poked too rapidly at keys on the computer. "I had the whole report right here just a second ago."

"Just tell me how it's going," said Gates. "I don't need the full report."

Wistol glanced up again at the chairman. He saw Rin alert and regarding him quizzically. Wistol snapped his gaze downward again at his computer, but he was too late. Rin was up and walking around the table toward him.

"Hey, come back here," ordered Gates.

Behind him Macklam stood up quietly from his seat against the wall.

"I said get back here," Gates repeated.

Rin looked back over his shoulder at Gates, who sat poised. He looked back at Macklam, poised. Rin returned to sit beside the billionaire chairman.

"It's definitely still growing," Albert Wistol rushed out. "In fact it's growing by a lot. I'll find the full report in just a second here but I know for a fact that Foundation awareness has increased, oh, I don't want to say by exactly how much until I find the actual report here, but I know from looking at it before that it's grown quite a bit. It's growing at a real good rate. I'm sure of that because I looked at it just a little while ago." Wistol recognized that he was speaking too much, but he couldn't plug the words as they gushed.

"That's exactly how we positioned it," said Osborne. "Now, with the Foundation high on everybody's mind, it's going to be there in the background behind everything you say. So this is perfect timing. This is the perfect time to get into something that's, you know, at a higher level, because now the Foundation's going to be there whether you mention it or not."

While Osborne spoke, Wistol scolded himself: *if I can just shut up. If I can stop talking right now – maybe they won't ask me anymore questions now. Maybe now I'm all done and I can just sit here. If I don't move again he won't see me.*

"Now you can talk about a dozen different things," Osborne went on. "Go in a dozen different directions and it won't matter, because now we've put the Foundation in the background of everything you talk about."

"But we have to keep it simple," advised Cynthia Boyd. "The simpler, the better. We should stick to one theme. One idea. It can still be a big idea. I'm not saying that the theme has to be simple or small or anything. But we can't do a dozen things. If you talk about a bunch of different topics instead of just one topic, it's not going to have the impact. If you want to make a strong statement, we have to stick to just one theme."

"Right," Osborne joined. "We just need that one big theme, that one value we stand for more than anything else."

"I need it to be quantitative too. Not just qualitative," said Gates. "I don't want to just state the thing and explain why it's important. These are Harvard graduates, after all. They all want to go out and fix the world. I need to give them a way to do that. An objective: something that can be aimed at and accomplished. Just like we do here. Just like we learned in running the businesses: identify and define the problem, lay out a plan of action, measure your success. Those same three steps we always lay out here with the business. I have to give them a plan like that."

"Right," Osborne said. "We can tell them how to accomplish, you know, that one big value."

"But how do you accomplish a value?" asked Boyd.

"First we need to decide what that value is," said Gates.

"Okay," Boyd replied, "what's your number one value?"

During the pause the followed, everyone but Albert Wistol scanned thoughtfully left and right around the table. Wistol remained still, with his eyes rigidly locked on the screen of the laptop computer pulled in tightly near his chest.

"It has to be justice," said Gates. "I mean *world* justice. Justice for every person in the world. For every person alive."

"As in 'liberty and justice for all?'" Osborne asked.

"No. Not American justice. This is Harvard. It has to mean justice for everyone in the world."

"Right. Everyone in the world. You can't go any higher than that," Osborne said.

"It makes a statement that has the highest impact anyone can make," Gates elaborated.

"I agree one-hundred percent," said Osborne.

"It's certainly lofty," said Cynthia Boyd. "But how do you translate that into a speech? We can do it. I mean, people talk about justice all the time. Especially at times like these. I mean, especially at graduation ceremonies. But don't forget: you said you want something concrete. Something you can take action on. You want a plan."

"The speech can be about taking action to achieve justice," Osborne cut in.

"But let's think about this before we go too far," continued Cynthia Boyd. "Because we also have to consider the audience. We should be mindful of what they want to hear. What's the audience going to find most interesting and also most useful. Time and time again, Bill, it comes up that what people want to hear from you is business. They want to hear how to be successful in business."

"But this is Harvard," Osborne said.

Boyd turned to Wistol, still locked on his computer screen.

"Albert, what do you find," she asked him. "Don't you find that there's still a very strong stream of interest in hearing about Bill's business success? Especially from young people like this who are just getting started?"

"But that's exactly what we're trying to change," Osborne protested emphatically. "We're trying to move Bill's identity beyond that now. We want to move beyond that whole big fascination with business and money and how he got all the money."

"I know that," said Boyd. "I'm just playing the devil's advocate. After all, he won't get another chance to speak at a Harvard graduation. I mean, they don't ask you twice. We just need to cover all the bases and make sure this one time is really good."

"That's why I'm aiming for the highest level value that's out there," Gates said.

"You can't get any higher than justice," Osborne repeated. "Al," he said to Wistol, "how does justice play in the Foundation talks Bill gives? It's come up a few times, hasn't it? On panels at Davos and I think some other places too? I think it's come up as a topic or a theme at least a few times when Bill has been presenting. Have you seen enough out there in the media to say how it plays when it enters the conversation? How justice plays?"

Wistol slapped fingers against keys on his close-in computer. *Just don't look up,* he said to himself. He pressed and daubed as if an urgent answer lie hidden inside the machine, as if his frantic finger-strokes and his anxious, buggy stare at the screen would reveal mysteries that answered Frank Osborne's question, as if the question itself possessed so much vital urgency that Wistol had to turn his whole self over to its answer. He strained at concentration. Inside his mind the name *Rin* taunted him rigorously, the word repeating itself uncontrollably, *Rin Rin Rin Rin.*

"Just tell me what you think," said Osborne. "I mean, you don't have to call up a formal report or anything."

"I'm just trying to find…" Wistol started.

"We need to keep this meeting moving," said Gates.

"I just thought that getting a good grip on the popularity of justice would help us to, you know, get started on your speech," Osborne said in defense.

"I don't care how popular it is," said Gates. "I just want it to have a high moral impact. It has to put us above the crowd. Cindy can make it compelling. She can make them listen. But it has to have a high moral content."

Wistol's spine and his fingers relaxed imperceptibly in sudden relief. *I don't have to talk now,* he gushed in his head. *Rin Rin Rin Rin Rin the dog.*

"Well, we already said that you can't get any higher than justice," Osborne went on.

Cynthia Boyd cut in, "but we still need to remember that it has to be part of a speech. I mean, no matter how important justice is to everybody, if you want it to have impact it still has to be presented in a way that grabs everybody. A concept like justice is pretty abstract. I mean, it's pretty obtuse. What can you really say about it other than what it is and why it's important? Can you talk about how we can make more justice? I guess you can, but I'm not so sure that will give you an address with a lot of impact. It might get too fuzzy for that."

"You mean we should bring it back down to earth," said Gates.

"That's always been your own rule," Boyd answered.

"So how do you make justice more concrete," Gates wondered out loud.

"Well," offered Osborne, "you can talk about the thing that makes justice. What about equality: the idea that we're all equal?"

"It's kind of the same problem," said Boyd. "It's still kind of vague. I mean, we all know what equality is, but it's hard to talk about it unless you speak in very abstract terms. And, again, that just doesn't make for a good speech. For a good speech we need something that moves. Something that points somewhere. Like a problem pointing to a solution. That's the only way we can get to Bill's three steps."

"Then all we need to do is turn equality into a problem that we can find a solution for," Osborne offered.

"Equality is not a problem," said Gates. "The problem is *in*equality."

"Of course," said Osborne. "That's a big, big problem."

"How does that sound, Cindy?" Gates asked. "Is inequality easier to work with?"

"Yeah. I think I can shape that into a good speech," said Cindy Boyd. "It lets me follow our usual pattern, and we already know that works. As long as I can start out with a large, identifiable problem, we can move it to a discussion of the solution, and then to the metrics portion to test if the solution is working. Our usual three steps should work very well with inequality."

"They can lead us to equality, as in 'all men are created equal,'" Osborne put in.

"Yeah, well maybe" mused Gates. "But that sounds awfully American. I want this to have a really large impact. It needs more of an international flavor. It's not enough just to have an impact. It's got to have an impact on the right people. Maybe equality and inequality isn't the word to use."

"How about inequity?" speech writer Cindy Boyd asked. "I can use inequity and still approach it the same way, still address the same problem."

"Inequity," Gates repeated, canting his head and turning his eyes upward toward the ceiling. "That sounds better. Yeah, let's use inequity."

"It's a really good word," said Boyd. "It's basically synonymous with inequality, but it just doesn't get used as much. You don't hear it all the time the way you hear inequality. That will make it stand out more. It will make it more memorable. It will make the speech much more memorable."

Suddenly Rin was up, unaccountably walking around the table with his nose twitched toward tremulous Albert Wistol.

Wistol began immediately to quaver and spew. He all but shouted out, "Inequity is a good word." He gulped. "It's just the right word we should use. It gets the message."

"Hey," said Gates to the dog. "Get back here."

But Rin continued to step inquisitively around the table toward Al Wistol. As he passed Cindy Boyd, she placed her hand lightly on Rin's back and let him walk beneath her palm.

"You're such a pretty boy," she said.

"Hey," Gates said again, this time standing. "Rin! I said get back here. Rin!"

"Rin," warned Macklam sharply from his seat against the wall.

"I'll handle it," said Gates, who now was stepping after Rin.

"Don't let him over here," clapped out Wistol. He stood up abruptly in panic, pushing back his chair so suddenly that it tipped and crashed with a whump as its back hit the floor. Rin flinched at the thud. He reeled backward a step. In the dog's hesitation, Gates scuffed to his side and scooped a hand toward his collar. But Rin leered away from the descending arm, causing Gates to miss the first grab. He caught the collar on the second swat, scooping his fingers beneath it and grasping Rin firmly enough to turn him back to his seat, chastened.

"I don't like dogs," Albert Wistol burbled in explanation. "I mean, I like 'em okay. Dogs are good animals and everything. I just get real nervous around them."

"This might be time for a biscuit," Macklam said quietly to Gates after he settled in his chair. But instead of pulling a treat from the pouch, Gates simply patted Rin's head.

"You could see that it wasn't going to hurt you," Gates shot toward Wistol.

"I know," he replied. "I just get real nervous. Dogs make me real nervous. It's just when they come real close to me. He was coming right over here."

"You see that sometimes," Macklam said quietly to Gates. "It's just a phobia. There's nothing he can do about it."

"You don't have to disrupt the whole meeting just because you're afraid of the dog," said Gates. "You ought to get used to it. We've got a whole bunch of dogs around here now."

"I'm sorry," said Wistol. "I really hate being this way."

"Come on, Al, you've got to get back on focus now." lectured Franklin Osborne. "We're talking about our two biggest projects this season. They're huge. We have to do this now. Right now. We can't mess anything up. We were just getting somewhere with Harvard. Inequity. We just decided inequity is the fundamental value for Bill's address at Harvard next month."

"Inequity's not a value," put in Cindy Boyd. "It's the problem that gets in the way of justice and equality. Those are the values."

"Right," said Osborne. "That's what I mean. Inequity's the problem. That's where we were when Al got us all jumbled up."

"We're way off the agenda now," said Gates.

"No, actually, I think we're okay," said Cindy Boyd, scrambling to make a defense for Wistol. "I mean, I think we were just about done anyway. Weren't we? Bill wants a problem-solving speech. I can do that if we work with the inequity theme. If we agree that that's the topic."

"It's a huge problem," said Osborne.

"Right," said Boyd. "I can work with that just fine. I can work with inequity – it's such a great word – and give it our usual, three-part construction, just like you want, Bill. Like we do with other things around here:

define the problem, develop a plan to fix it, and then measure your results. That will make the speech concrete. It'll stand out for that. It'll stand out a lot because it's not airy and it's not too lofty like all those other Harvard commencement speeches we've been boning up on. Now it's just a matter of me getting a first draft to you. So I don't think we're off the agenda. I think we're pretty-much done. I don't think there's any need for Albert to sit through this any longer."

Her urgings ended the meeting after a small summary discussion. When Osborne, Boyd and Wistol left the round conference room, Reggie Macklam stepped up from the wall and sat down at the table with Gates.

"It looks like we had that interruption you wanted to avoid at all costs," Macklam said.

"I'm not so sure about that," Gates replied. "We had an interruption. That's for sure. But I'm not so sure it's Rin that caused it. I don't mind so much that he got up. There's nothing really wrong with him moving around as long as he doesn't get in anyone's way. And he didn't, really. It was Al Wistol that caused the interruption. I've never seen anybody get so worked up just because a dog is coming toward them."

"It's like I said before," explained Macklam, "it's just a phobia. It's just the way God made some people and there's really nothing he can do about it. But I have to say, that fella has it worse than anyone I've ever seen."

"It's just a dog," said Gates. "He ought to have more control. I can't blame Rin for that. It looked to me like he was just being curious."

"That's all it was," agree Macklam. "He certainly wasn't trying to stir things up. Still, it caused a pretty big disruption of your meeting here."

"But he wasn't hard to control," Gates countered. "I'd have to say that he even listened to me, especially at first. And at the end when I had to get up, again, that was Al's fault so getting so worked up. He might as well have been calling Rin over. You could see that."

"So you don't count today as a deal breaker?"

"No. In fact, I'm pretty pleased with how I handled him."

"You're sure? Because now's the time to decide, because the next thing coming up is your thinking week. You'll be alone with Rin then. I won't be there at all, at least not while the two of you are with that reporter."

"I know," said Gates. "But it won't be for that long. He's coming to observe for something like four hours, five hours. We'll talk some too, of course. I'll have to show him what I do. It'll probably be more like a meeting than anything else. But I can handle Rin at the same time. From what I've seen, he'll mostly just lie down and sleep. If he gets in the way I can just drag him off to another room."

"That's right. And I can come get him as soon as the reporter finishes. As soon as he leaves, I mean. You only need him there for the day, while you're, you know, in the public eye – or in the reporter's eye, anyway. After that, there's no one to see you. Do you really stay there for the whole week?"

"Right. Well, for five days."

"And you spend all that time reading those, what do you call them, research reports and such?"

"Yeah, pretty much. There's other things too. But there's no meetings like the one we just had here. It's a week without any scheduled meetings."

"And you're there all alone for that time?"

"Right. There's the cook and the housekeeper, of course. But there's no other Microsoft people there. No other executives or anything."

"Sounds like a vacation," said Macklam.

"Except that I have all those research proposals to get through. I write comments on every one."

"Okay," said Macklam. "I see what you mean. It's not a vacation because you bring work with you. I guess when I go on vacation I don't bring a dog with me."

"I'll have my dog with me," quipped Gates.

"So maybe it will be a vacation for him," Macklam grinned. "Not that he needs one. I get him out as much as I can when he's not spending time with you. I have to say that he's doing real well. Rin and his little friend Ester are getting on just fine. I can't say the same about those other four – those four breeding males we're keeping for your missus. We're going to try clearing the female out to see if they improve at all. We'll get her away from them for just a day to see if there's any difference. I just have to figure out where to keep her."

"Why don't you just send her to the lodge with Rin for the day," said Gates.

"What? You mean now you want two dogs?"

"Not necessarily. But it can't be much harder than having just one. And if one dog is good for my image, then two should look even better."

"So now you want two?"

"It's just for the day. For only one day I don't think that two can be much more difficult to handle than just one."

"Sometimes they can. But I don't think that will be the case with Amanda. All in all she's a very timid girl, and she shouldn't give you any trouble at all."

"Then bring her along with Rin."

"I will. But first I have to say that I'm impressed by how you make decisions. Surprised a little bit too, I think. You're certainly bold. I give you credit for that. Not much more than an hour ago you were hedging about having even Rin around. Now you turn a little corner with him and you're ready to take on two."

"I believe in committing one-hundred percent to a plan once I see that it's going to work. Today I could see that I can make Rin behave like he's mine. Everyone assures me that having him here will be good for my image."

"That's great," Macklam beamed. "As of today, young Rin here is officially Bill Gates' dog."

CHAPTER 6

Dremmel, Blake and Web lounged in easy comfort at the far edge of their outdoor enclosure, stretching their bodies in the dappled shade cast by the tree that arched above them from Amanda's adjacent yard. Georgie was alone in the partitioned area that the four boys shared inside the building. He padded into the den next to his, where Web ate and slept. Georgie nosed around Web's bed. He turned up the edges of the mattress to see if anything might hide underneath. He poked into Web's empty food dish. He took a single lap from the water bowl. Georgie stood high against the back wall, trying to see over the top of it. It was a partition wall that ran up only part way to the ceiling. But it was the same wall the ran along the back of all the dogs' sleeping dens, too high for Georgie to breach. He stepped down gingerly and padded out of Web's room through the door that Debbie Green left always open. He stepped into the next cell in the line, where Blake ate and slept.

Outside, Blake stood up and resettled himself. He looked carefully around the compound, peering through the woven fencing at the three open yards that stood beside the one he shared with Dremmel, Georgie and Web.

"I wonder where Amanda is," he quizzed. "She must be inside. I don't see her anywhere out here."

"Where's Georgie?" said Dremmel with a start, rising up on sudden alert.

"He must be inside too," answered Blake.

"Why isn't he out here with us?" Dremmel asked.

"I don't know."

"What's he doing in there?"

"I don't know."

"I don't trust him," said Dremmel.

"Georgie said you don't trust anyone," said Web with open innocence.

"He *would* say that," Dremmel snubbed.

"I wonder when Amanda's coming out," said Blake.

"You can bet that when she does, Georgie will be out here too," Dremmel said.

"I've been talking to her a lot," said Blake. "She likes me. I know she does."

"It doesn't matter who she likes," said Dremmel. "She's not Bill Gates. Bill Gates is all that matters. We've been through all that before. She's here because he wants her here, same as the rest of us. She could go too, you know. It's up to Bill Gates."

"Everything is up to Bill Gates," repeated Web.

"I can do everything Bill Gates wants me to do," Blake said.

"Here comes Amanda," Web announced.

Blake sprang up and stepped quickly along the fence to meet her. "Hi there. It's me again," he said to her through the wire. "I was just wondering where you were."

"I was inside," she said.

"I know," said Blake. "I was just gonna come over here and call you. It's a beautiful day out here. I was gonna see if you wanted to come out so we can talk some more."

"Sure," said Amanda. "What do you want to talk about?"

"I don't know. Nothing really. I mean, I just wanted to talk to you. We can talk about anything you want to."

She giggled. "Well, I want to talk about whatever you want to talk about," Amanda replied.

"We were just talking about Bill Gates over there," Blake said.

"Why?" she asked. "Is he coming here?"

"No. I mean, I don't think so. I mean, I guess he could be coming here, 'cause he can go anywhere he wants to. But he's never been here before. None of us have ever even seen him. You haven't seen him, have you?"

"No," answered Amanda. "I only know what you guys told me about him."

"Yeah. That's Dremmel. He's talking about him all the time. He was talking about him just now. That's what I meant. I was over there with Dremmel and he started talking about Bill Gates again. But we don't have to talk about him if you don't want to. I was just saying that Bill Gates was what Dremmel was talking about."

"Dremmel knows everything about Bill Gates," Amanda said.

"Well, yeah, I guess so. I mean, he sure thinks he does. But don't you get tired of hearing about him all the time? I mean, that's all Dremmel ever talks about."

Amanda giggled.

"I mean, I like Bill Gates too," Blake said. "Everybody does. We have to like him. But that doesn't mean we have to talk about him all the time. I do everything he wants me to do, just like I'm supposed to. Maybe Dremmel should work on that more, work on being good, instead of just worrying about it all the time."

While Blake and Amanda prated, Dremmel and Web watched the conversation as they stayed in the comfortable shade at the edge of their outdoor enclosure.

"That Blake really likes to talk to Amanda," Web said.

"Of course he does," said Dremmel.

"I wonder what they're talking about?"

"I know just what they're talking about," Dremmel said. "I know what he's up to. He's trying to get in good with her. He wants to be the one who gets to marry her. That's exactly what he wants. He figures that way he'll get to stay here for sure. He figures if he's married to Amanda, there's no way he'll disappear. There's no way Bill Gates will let anything like that happen to him."

"But you said Bill Gates gets to pick who marries her," said Web.

"Of course he does," Dremmel answered. "Bill Gates picks everything in the end. But he's not going to decide on someone she doesn't like. He wants her to like him. That's why there's four of us here to choose from. If he was going to pick just anyone he wouldn't need to have us all here. You have to think about these things. Why would he have us all here if just anyone would do? He wants to see who's best for her, that's why. He wants to see which one of us she's going to like the most. You know: be the most happiest with. That's the one he'll pick. That's why Blake is trying to get in good with her. He wants to marry her so he'll be sure to get to stay here. He doesn't want to just disappear."

"Like Big Gandhi?" Web asked.

"Just like Big Gandhi. He was here and now he's gone and nobody knows what happened to him. That can happen to me and you too, you know."

"I know," said Web.

"The only way to fix that is to get in good with Amanda," Dremmel said. "The only way is to be the one that Amanda likes. Then Bill Gates will like you too. Then you'll get to stay here for certain. That's why Blake's over there. Look at how he's showing off to her. Look at him. As if that's a big deal. I can do all that stuff. All those things he's always bragging about, I can do them too. He's no big deal."

"But Amanda likes Blake."

"No she doesn't," Dremmel scoffed. "He's just running up to her all the time and getting in everybody else's way. Georgie, too. The two of them are hogging her. That's all. They're both just trying to be with her all the time. But that doesn't mean she likes them. Not yet, anyway. I can beat them at that game. I can make sure she chooses me to be her husband, no matter what those two do."

"How can you do that?" asked Web.

"I can do things that they can't do," said Dremmel. "I can figure things out that they can't figure out. With all the studying I've done, I'm smarter than they are. A lot smarter. I know things that they don't know anything about – things they never even heard about. After all the studying I've done, I can show her who the smart one really is. I can show her I'm the best. I can show her I'm better than Georgie, that's for sure. With all his primping and preening and all his smiling and his cooing around. With all my studying and the way I put things together and figure them out, I'm way better than Georgie. Blake too. Forget all his sports, all his running and jumping and everything like that. Forget all that big talking he does. He thinks he's a sports star. He thinks he does everything just right. He thinks he's safe because he follows all the commands and everything. I'll show him up for sure. I'll make him look like a real idiot. Amanda won't think too much of him then."

"But Blake's all right," protested Web.

Dremmel peered carefully at Web, assessing him.

"Sure he's all right," Dremmel said. "I don't have anything against Blake. It's not about that. It's about Amanda and doing what's right for her. What's best for her. You want what's best for Amanda, don't you?"

"Sure I do, Dremmel. You know I do. Everybody wants that."

"It's what Bill Gates wants: Amanda's welfare," said Dremmel. "Debbie Green, too. They all want what's best for Amanda. So we have to make sure of that too. Right?"

"Well, yeah. Right," said Web.

"Why don't you go over there and see what they're talking about," Dremmel said. "I'd really like to know what he's telling her. But don't tell 'em I sent you. Just act like you went over there on your own. In fact, act like you're just walking past. Like you're heading inside to see what Georgie's doing. Yeah, that's it: tell 'em you're just going inside to see Georgie. I want to know what he's up to anyway. You can stop and see Blake and Amanda but then go inside to find Georgie. Let me know what he's up to, too. You can see what Blake's telling Amanda and you can see what Georgie's up to inside. Just don't tell any of 'em I sent you."

"Okay," said Web, "I can go see Georgie."

"Don't tell 'em though."

"Don't worry, Dremmel. I won't tell 'em you sent me."

Blake and Amanda were still buzzing brightly by the fence when Web walked up to them.

"Hey, what are you guys doing?" he asked them.

"We're just talking," said Blake.

"We're waiting for Debbie Green to come out," Amanda added. "Blake is going to show her that when he jumps up here he can reach that bar at the top of this tall fence here."

"You can reach that?" asked Web.

"Sure he can," said Amanda. "He just showed me."

"I wonder if I can reach it too," Web said.

"It's really high," Amanda offered.

Web stepped backward two steps. He bounded forward and sprang upward at the fence, swatting the top bar that capped the high poles supporting the chainlink.

"Wow," he said. "That really is high."

Blake said, "I can reach it without a running start."

"Really?" said Web.

"He just showed me," Amanda answered.

From a standstill Web sprang upward, stretching, but just missing the top bar.

"It's not so easy, is it?" said Blake.

"No," said Web. "That's really high."

"He's going to show Debbie Green," Amanda said.

"Is she coming out now?" Web asked them.

"Well, yeah. I mean, I guess she is," said Blake. "She comes out here all the time. But we're not just waiting for her. We're talking. We have a lot of things we talk about."

"Really?" said Web. "Like what?"

"Well, I don't know. Nothing really. I mean, there's just a whole bunch of different things we like to talk about."

Amanda said, "Blake won a lot of races. He was number one in his class. Not just in racing, but in other things too, like frisbee and like jumping. Jumping high *and* jumping far. That's why he can touch the top bar. Because he's number one in sports."

"Is that what you're talking about?" Web asked.

"Other things too," said Amanda.

"Like what?"

"Just things," shot Blake. "Different things. What's it to you anyway," he sneered toward Web. "What do you care what we're talking about. I don't go around asking you what you're doing, do I? What about you and Dremmel? You were over there for a long time together. What if I ask you what you two were talking about for so long?"

"We weren't really talking about anything," said Web. "Mostly we were just resting. Dremmel wanted ... well, he just talked about Bill Gates a little bit."

"Dremmel knows everything about Bill Gates," Amanda said.

"I was just going inside to see Georgie when I ran into you guys," explained Web.

"Then why don't you keep going," said Blake. "Why don't you go bother Georgie and leave us alone."

"Okay, okay," rushed Web. "I'm going."

Inside the building, Georgie had moved into the room where Dremmel stayed. Web found him nosing over a shelf that ran above Dremmel's bed. Georgie stiffened when he saw Web enter the room.

"Hey, there you are Georgie," Web beamed at him. "Whacha doin'?"

"Me? Nothin' really. I was just on my way out to see what you were doin', Web. What's goin' on with you?"

"Ah, nuthin' really. I was just talkin' to Blake and Amanda out there. We did some jumping."

"Amanda's out there?"

"She came out a little while ago."

"Man, Web, you should of come to get me sooner."

"Sooner? What for?"

"So I could get out there with Amanda."

"Oh, that's okay. Blake is already out there with her."

"Figures. I wonder what that asshole is doing with her now."

"Hey," said Web, "Blake's okay."

"I know. I was just joking. I just wonder what they're doing together."

"They're just talking. They did some jumping, too. They're waiting for Debbie Green to come out so they can show her how high Blake can jump. He makes it all the way to that top bar along the top of the fence. A little higher and he could probably pull himself over. He was number one in jumping."

"Oh yeah? Number one, eh? That's what he says, anyway."

"I believe him," said Web. "I tried jumping that high and it's really hard. I made it after a running start. I think I could do it from standing, too, if I tried just a little bit harder. But it's really hard."

"When's Debbie Green coming out?" Georgie asked.

"I don't know. They're just waiting for her. What are you doin' here in Dremmel's room?" Web asked him.

"Me? Oh, nuthin', really. I just came in to see if Dremmel was around. I was just goin' outside. I came in to see if he wanted to come. I just wish I knew Amanda was out there sooner."

"Why? You like to talk to her too?"

"Hell yes," said Georgie. "I like talkin' to her just fine. But that's not all I'd like to do. The way she looks, there's a lot of other things I'd like to do to her."

"Amanda's not like that," said Web.

"Oh, really?" said Georgie. "We'll just have to see about that. One thing's for sure: she's the hottest looking lady I've ever seen. I keep trying to get alone with her, but every time I see her, Blake comes trotting over. I can never get alone with her without Blake coming around."

"Blake really likes to talk to her," Web said.

"Who doesn't? But he doesn't have to talk to her all the time. He needs to give the rest of us a chance, too. Hell, he wouldn't even know what to do with her anyway."

"Dremmel says we have to make sure she's happy, because that's what Bill Gates wants."

"Oh, I'd make her happy all right," said Georgie. "I just need to get her alone."

"Bill Gates picks that," Web reminded him.

"I know. I know. And he's got Debbie Green looking around down here all the time for him. She never leaves us alone. I can't do anything without her getting in the way. Don't you wish she'd just leave us alone for a while?"

"She gives us our food," said Web.

"Yeah, yeah. I just gotta find a way to get alone with Amanda. If I could get Blake away from her, or maybe meet her someplace where Blake can't get to . . .. See the wall back there in the back of the bedroom? It only goes part way up. See how it's open at the top, how it doesn't go up to the ceiling? If I can figure out some way to get over it and get out on the other side, I bet I can get inside Amanda's place."

"You mean go over on Debbie Green's side?" asked Web.

"Just for a minute," Georgie answered. "Just till I can make my way to Amanda's. Till I can get inside Amanda's place and be alone with her. But I got to get over this wall first. You can go anywhere once you get to that side. That's why Debbie Green won't let us in there. That's why she keeps us shut out of there all the time. Once we get over on that side, we can go anywhere."

"I don't know if they'd like that."

"Well of course they wouldn't like it. That's why they don't let us out. But, come on, Web, don't you want to get out there and do something?

Don't you want to at least have a look around? I bet we could have all sorts of fun out there. Don't you?"

"Well, sure, Georgie. If you think we could. But I don't see how you're gonna get over that wall."

"Yeah, I don't know yet either. I've been trying to figure it out but so far I haven't come up with anything. That's why I'm tellin' you about it now: I think we're gonna have to work together. I think maybe with two of us, I can come up with some way we can work together to get over and get out of here. Just for a while, I mean. I'll figure out some way to get out and then get back in. You know: to come and go."

"Maybe Dremmel can help us," said Web. "He's real good at figuring things out."

"No, not Dremmel," rushed Georgie. "Whatever you do, don't say anything to Dremmel. Don't say anything to anybody. This is just me and you. You can't tell anybody. We don't want Dremmel tagging along and the last thing we want is Blake. Don't say anything to Amanda, either. Whatever you do, don't say anything to her."

"But I thought you're going to visit her?"

"Oh, I'll visit her. You can be sure of that. But I want it to be a surprise. Besides, she might say something to somebody else. This has to be a secret. That goes for you too, Web. You can't say a word to anyone else. I'm only tellin' you because you and me are friends. I mean, you're my best friend. That's why we do so much together. So you promise me you won't say a word?"

"I promise, Georgie. I won't tell anyone."

"You gotta remember. I mean, you can't let something slip out by accident."

"I'll remember, Georgie."

"Good. We'll keep it our secret. Just give me a little time to figure something out. I'll let you know when I do. In the meantime just forget all about it, okay? Don't even try to think about it or anything, or you might let something slip out. Okay? In fact, we'd better quit talkin' about it now or somebody's gonna get suspicious. Hey, is Amanda still out there?"

Web turned out of Dremmel's room and stepped to the door that led outside.

"She's still out here with Blake," he called back to Georgie.

"Still with Blake? Ask me if I'm surprised."

But as Georgie and Web approached them outside, they saw immediately that Amanda and Blake had snapped off their playful chatter. They remained facing each other still, on opposite sides of the fence that divided their yards, but both Blake and Amanda now looked suddenly detached and transported, as though the landscape they looked at had spontaneously changed.

"Hey," Web blew at them, "aren't you guys jumping anymore?"

"Debbie Green was just out here," said Blake.

"She was?" said Web. "I didn't even see her."

"I have to go away tomorrow," said Amanda.

"You're going away?" Georgie exclaimed.

"I'm going away to be with Bill Gates."

"But no one's been with Bill Gates. No one's ever even seen Bill Gates," Georgie protested.

"I guess I'll see him tomorrow."

"Tomorrow? You're going away tomorrow?" Georgie rued.

Dremmel saw their excited clatter and trotted over from his place in the shade.

"Amanda's going away," Web announced to him. "It's just like you said, Dremmel. She's going away tomorrow. She'll be gone and we'll never see her again."

"No, it's not like that," Amanda explained a little emphatically. "I'm only going away for a few days. That's what Debbie Green said. She said I'd be gone for a couple of days is all. I think it's just for one night. Or maybe it's two."

"She's going to be with Bill Gates," Web explained.

"She's not going alone, either," said Blake. He motioned with a nod in the direction of the far enclosure where Rin lived with Ester. "He's going too," Blake announced.

"Who's going?" Georgie demanded.

"He is," Blake answered. "That non-breed who lives over there with that old lady. He's going too. That's what Debbie Green told us just now."

"But I thought he was gone," Georgie said. "We stopped seeing him and I thought he was just gone now. We all thought that. We all said good-riddance."

"He's not gone," said Blake. "He goes out during the days and that's why we never see him. But at night he comes back here to sleep. He's been coming back all along. That's what Debbie Green just told Amanda and me."

"He spends the whole day with Bill Gates," Amanda added.

"He does!" gaped Georgie. "That guy over there who lives with that non-breed? He's just a non-breed himself. He spends all day with Bill Gates?"

"That's what Debbie Green told us."

"I don't believe it!"

"That's what she said."

The five of them stood silently, pondering.

"Are you sure about this?" Dremmel asked after a moment.

"Completely sure," Blake answered. "Debbie Green was just here. You saw her. She told Amanda she has to get all cleaned up and ready today because tomorrow she's going away with that nonnie over there to a place where Bill Gates will be."

"What place?" Dremmel demanded.

"A special place where Bill Gates goes," Amanda replied. "He goes there alone and Rin will be there too because Rin is Bill Gates' dog."

"But why do you have to go?" Georgie asked her.

"I don't know," Amanda answered.

"Because Bill Gates wants her to," Dremmel ventured.

"Debbie Green never said why," Blake put in.

"She said it's for thinking," Amanda elaborated. "Debbie Green said it's a special place Bill Gates goes just for thinking."

"If it's for thinking then I think that Dremmel should go," Web said.

"She told you that nonnie over there is Bill Gates' dog?" Dremmel asked.

"That's what she said," Blake responded. "She said Rin is Bill Gates' dog. Debbie Green said that. She said he's with him every day and now he knows Bill Gates really good."

"That nonnie," scorned Georgie in an expanding yap of dislike and disbelief.

"He's Bill Gates' dog," Blake repeated with anger apparent this time. "That's why we don't see him here now. He comes back home to sleep but that's all. But now he'll be gone for a couple of nights because Bill Gates is going away. Amanda too. She'll be with him."

"I have to start getting ready," Amanda said. "I need to take a bath and everything so I'd better get started right away."

The four males stood silently while Amanda pattered away and disappeared through the door to her home. They stayed silent a moment longer. Blake dropped his head and kicked so his foot scuffed the ground. Georgie broke the silence, declaring in protest, "She'll be alone with that nonnie."

"When do they leave?" Dremmel asked.

"They leave tomorrow some time in the morning," Blake explained. "It's real far away so they'll be together for hours while Debbie Green drives them there. They'll stay there tomorrow night and the next day they'll be with Bill Gates. I think they come back on the day after that."

"Two nights!" Georgie cringed. "She'll be alone with that nonnie for two nights!"

"Or maybe even three," Blake corrected. "I'm not sure if they come back the day after tomorrow or if they stay another day. But even if they only stay two nights, it'll give him as much time to talk to her as I've had the whole time I've been here."

"I'm not gonna stand for this," fumed Georgie.

"What are you going to do?" Web asked him.

"I don't know yet."

"Don't worry," said Blake. "I'll take care of that Rin and then there'll be nothing to worry about."

"But how?" Web asked.

"I'll figure it out," Blake said.

The four of them stood silently again until finally Dremmel announced, "I've gotta get back to the shade." Georgie, Blake and Web silently watched Dremmel as he paced away. Then Web broke off and followed him.

Blake said: "I'm goin' inside the house to lie down."

"Me too," said Georgie.

When Dremmel and Web were alone in the shade at the far end of their yard, they remained silent through several long moments. Dremmel's mouth locked in a twisted grimace, awaiting words that his mind was unwilling to form. At last he muttered and almost moaned, "I don't believe it. This is awful. It's a disaster. This is worse than I ever thought it could be.

A lot worse." Words and even thought appeared to abandon him again. After a painful moment he declared, "I don't know what I'm going to do now."

"Maybe we should make friends with him," Web ventured.

"With who? With that nonnie over there?"

"Well, yeah. I mean, if he's Bill Gates' dog."

"He's not Bill Gates' dog," Dremmel insisted. "He can't be. There's got to be something else going on."

"Like what?" Web wondered.

"I don't know what," Dremmel snapped in annoyance. "I need some time to figure it out." He pondered a while. "What's that nonnie's name again?" Dremmel asked at last.

"It's Rin," answered Web. "Georgie said his name is Rin."

"Rin. Right. I won't forget that name again. Not if Rin is really Bill Gates' dog. But he can't be. Can he? I just can't figure this out. I need more time to think about it. If it's true, it changes everything I ever thought. It makes everything a lot worse. A whole lot worse. But it can't be true, can it? How can Rin be Bill Gates' dog? He's just a nonnie. He has no breeding at all. He lives in that little place over there. And now he's going away with Amanda? I never thought Bill Gates would put Rin with Amanda. I thought maybe he'd pick Blake. Maybe even Georgie. I figured there was a chance of that. But I never thought anything about that other guy. That Rin. I just can't figure it out. He doesn't have any breeding."

"Don't worry so much about it, Dremmel," said Web. "Didn't you hear Blake? He said he's going to take care of him. Georgie too. Both Blake and Georgie said they're going to put him in his place."

"Don't give me that," lashed Dremmel. "What are they gonna do? What *can* they do? They can't even get to him. Most of the time he's not even around. He's with Bill Gates, remember? And even if he was around, he's way over there and we're way over here. There's no way they can get there. There's no way they can get anywhere. There's no way they can get out of here to do anything. No way at all."

"But Georgie said…" Web started. He checked himself and glanced anxiously at Dremmel to see if his slip and his abrupt stop had registered.

"Georgie said what?" Dremmel demanded. "What about Georgie? What were you about to say?"

"I wasn't really gonna say anything," said Web.

"Yes you were," insisted Dremmel. "We were talking about getting out of here and you started to say something about Georgie. What is it? Can Georgie get out of here? Does he know a way? Is that what you were going to say?"

"No, Dremmel. I wasn't going to say that. I wasn't really gonna say anything. I wasn't. I was just, I was just, I don't know, I was just kind of wondering if maybe Georgie could figure out a way to get out of here."

"Why?" demanded Dremmel with hissing insistence. "Why would you wonder that? Does Georgie know a way to get out of here?"

"No. I mean, I don't know."

"Is he trying to get out?" Dremmel pushed. "Is that what was he doing in there?"

"No, Dremmel, he wasn't trying to get out. Not when I went in there just now."

"Then what was he doing?"

"Well, gee, I don't know. He wasn't doing anything. Not really. He was just coming out to see us right when I came in."

"What was he doing right before you came in?"

"I don't know, Dremmel. I guess he was resting. But right when I came in he was on his way out. That's just what he told me."

"As if we can trust anything he says," said Dremmel. "But if Georgie knows a way to get out of here, then you'd better tell me."

"He doesn't know, Dremmel. Honest. But you know Georgie: he might figure something out sooner or later."

"Yeah, I know Georgie. That's the last thing I need is him running around out there. It would ruin everything. We'd all be in for it then. If Georgie got out we'd be in so much trouble – we just can't let that happen. Got that? There's no way we can let Georgie get out of here. He'd get us in so much trouble. Blake too. We have to watch him the same as Georgie. 'Cause who knows what he's gonna try to do, too. When you were over there a little while ago I saw him trying to jump over to Amanda's yard. If we're not careful he's going to get us all in trouble, just like Georgie. The two of them will make us all look bad. We'd disappear for sure after that. We gotta keep 'em in line. If Georgie figures out a way to get out of here, you'd better tell me about it."

"I will," said Web.

"You'd better."

"I will. I promise I will."

"That's the last thing I need is Georgie out there. It's bad enough now with this Rin. But if Georgie gets out... I just can't let that happen. I've got to keep him in line and make sure he doesn't do anything that messes things up for me."

CHAPTER 7

Debbie Green stopped the long, lumbering, Chevrolet Suburban sport-utility vehicle at the turnoff to the driveway that wended toward the lodge where Gates and Macklam waited. The dashboard navigation system had led her here, but the entry to the drive looked more secluded and nondescript, more overgrown, less obvious and less ostentatious than she had expected. She looked hard again at the illuminated map on the big wagon's dashboard. This had to be the place, she thought. She plunged the long vehicle into the wrap of bracken and underbrush and tall-arching limbs that closed around the tight gravel drive. Branch tips scraped and scored the dust that settled on the side of the Suburban as Debbie jounced it cautiously deeper along the drive until at last the pathway opened to a broader, more accommodating roadbed with wide shoulders of shorn lawn on each side. Ahead she saw the lodge. Again it was less ostentatious than she had antici-pated. But still it stood as large as a family-sized suburban home. She saw the deep, glistening finger of the crystalline lake that touched near the back of the lodge. Or maybe that was the front, she wondered.

Macklam met her outside to take Amanda and Rin from the vehicle and settle them in the lodge. He told Debbie Green she could wait outside. He had set up arrangements in the lodge already, he told her. If she needed a warmer jacket or a sweater she would find them hanging in a foyer just inside the door here. She could wear what she wanted, whatever she found there, he said, but she would find the wait more pleasant outside by the lake where the view across the clear water was tranquil and settling. Macklam and Debbie would leave together in the sport-utility, he told her, as soon as he finished settling Amanda and Rin inside the lodge with Gates.

After Macklam and Green departed, Amanda and Rin stayed silently with Bill Gates in the room that Gates called the study. He left them alone when the reporter from the New York Times arrived and, as planned, Gates walked outside to greet the man.

Rin stood up and watched them attentively through a window. As the two men began to stroll around a side of the building toward the back of the house, Rin shifted and pranced to pick them up through another window.

"Look," he said to Amanda. "Bill Gates is taking that other man around to look at the lake."

Amanda stepped cautiously and stretched to see out the window without approaching Rin too closely.

"I wish he'd take us out there too," said Rin. "That water looks fantastic. Wouldn't you love to go swimming here?"

"I don't know," said Amanda. "I don't know if he'd want us to do that."

"Oh, don't worry. He'd let you know. If he didn't want you to go in the water he'd tell you right away. You'd know what he wants and you don't have to wonder. Like now when he just went out. He said 'stay here,' so you know we're just going to stay in this room and wait. But, boy, it sure would be nice to get out there and get in that lake."

"Do you think he'll let you later?"

"I don't know. I guess he might but I really don't think so. Usually it's Macklam that takes me to do things like that. Usually with Bill Gates I just kind of stay."

"Stay where?"

"Stay wherever he is. That's where he wants me so I'm not going to argue."

"But what do you do?"

"I stay there. I mean, I don't really do much of anything. I sit down next to him and I just kind of stay there."

"But you're with him all day."

"Yep."

"Doesn't that get kind of boring?"

"Boring? I don't know. I never looked at it as boring. Because I get to be there for everything he does. You should see all the people that come to see him. All day. And all the things they ask him about. They want to know everything from him. Everything. They say what they're making and they tell him how much work they've done so far. And he tells them they should've done this and they shouldn't have done that and now what they need to do next. And they tell him about different monies they're giving. Where it all went and what it pays for and how much more is coming back and everything like that. They talk about that for hours. You should see all the people who come in to see him for all that kind of stuff. And they all just wait while he talks and they listen real carefully to everything he says and then most of the time they repeat what he says to make sure they know what he wants them to do. I sit right there with him for that. It's great."

"Do they do all of that indoors?" Amanda asked.

"Oh, yeah," Rin answered. "They're always in rooms. They have all sorts of rooms. Whenever I'm with Bill Gates I'm in one of his rooms. But I get out a lot with Macklam, too. A lot of times when Bill Gates is changing rooms, Macklam comes to get me. He's always around nearby. We talk a lot. He tells me I've been good. He tells me I need to get out for air and exercise and we walk together a lot of times in the trees and on some rocky paths I've found in the big open stretch of land that runs on forever just over that little hill you can see from where our houses are. Sometimes we go for miles back there because I think Macklam likes it as much as me. He says it's what we both need to do more often: to get out in the air with the trees and the big mossy rocks and everything. He says we're too cooped up so sometimes, when we have the time, we both go for an hour back there. Maybe longer. It's great."

"Debbie Green talks to me a lot," said Amanda.

"Yeah. She's around a lot of the time, too. Especially when I'm back at old Ester's house where I sleep. But Debbie Green is always rubbing up with everyone, so it doesn't mean too much."

"Yeah, I guess I know what you mean, because I've kind of noticed that too," said Amanda.

"You mean you've noticed the way that she talks?"

"Yeah. The voice that she uses sometimes. And how she tells everyone she loves them and she tells everyone they're special. So deep down you don't really feel very special because you know she says it to everyone."

"That's right," said Rin. "She's okay to talk to, but it's just not worth a whole lot."

They stood side by side peering quietly for a moment through the window as Gates gestured and pointed around the lake, speaking earnestly to the reporter in words they could not hear about the crystalline body.

"Do you think Macklam will take us swimming in there today?" Amanda asked Rin more eagerly.

"I don't know. He might. He's coming back here later to get us. But we're not going to stay here. He already said that. We'll stay someplace else, so I don't know if we'll be able to go for a swim in this lake or not. Maybe. It'll be up to Macklam. But it'll be great if we do."

"I think I'd really like it," she said.

"Hey, they're coming inside now," said Rin with new urgency. "We'd better be quiet for a while. He doesn't like it so much when we talk."

The two men entered the study briskly, in a file with Gates in the lead. He sat down behind the broad, airy desk in the room and directed the reporter to wheel up a chair so that Gates could, as he put it, show the reporter his general routine. The idea was simply to read through these things, Gates said as he pushed a high stack of bound papers and files across the desk top to show the man. They were idea summaries, he said. The papers came from people all over his company who had ideas for new projects or revised approaches or sudden departures and bold initiatives. Every one was different, Gates said. Some were grand and far-reaching while others were more narrowly focused. All of the ideas were speculative and required a lot more refinement. Few would ever come to anything. But which few? They all deserved consideration, he stressed. But too often they simply got lost in the maw of the world's biggest software company.

That was the problem he sought to resolve with his thinking week, Gates explained earnestly. He wanted to give every idea an airing, to help make the organization more innovative. So every year, he said, he had all the proposals collected from every corner of the company. He had them printed on paper, he explained, because even with a whole week of seclusion, he had so many summaries to get through that he couldn't risk any kind of a failure that might block him out of computer files. There were lots more than these, Gates said with a nod to the stack on his desk. These were just the ideas he needed to work through over the next several hours.

So he would read them all, he explained, and make notations on each report about what future action he felt was needed, indicating how much promise he thought an individual idea might hold, recommending avenues and approaches that might refine or advance an idea, and encouraging those idea-makers whom he deemed most deserving.

The whole process was fascinating, the reporter responded. But to make his article more vivid and vital and truly unique, he would need to learn details about some of the specific ideas, he said. He would need to summarize some representative samples and, importantly, he would need to see Gates' comments, so he could compellingly account for the thinking-week retreat of Bill Gates.

Of course, Gates agreed. He already understood that the reporter would need to get details. He had already assured him full access. The confidentially papers the reporter had signed, vetted by lawyers from both sides, from both the newspaper company and the software company, legally restricted the man to use the information for the article alone. The agreement gave Gates or his handlers authority to review the article before publication, to make sure it didn't let out any company secrets or, importantly, convey any spurious digs. In exchange, Gates emphasized, the reporter received unprecedented access. So of course Gates would show the man these papers, he said, and even explain his comments, after he worked through the batch.

The next several hours passed largely in silence, with Gates shifting here and there, moving from chair to lounger to couch in various corners of the study, to maintain his comfort. In each position he read very quickly, marking the papers occasionally, scratching bold pronouncements when he finished each one. The reporter stayed in a single chair backed against the wall that faced the water. He wrote out notes, moving his hand slowly and pausing for long moments – sometimes very long moments – to peer around the room between each notation. He looked at the desk and then wrote down a note on his pad. He peered for a long period at the rows of shelves that striped the wall adjacent to the wall where he sat, lingering seemingly on each object upon the shelves, the books, the binders, the paraphernalia like vintage computer chips and vacuum tubes, a clock, even a fishing hat. He gazed up at the ceiling. The reporter rose very quietly and stepped to a window that looked out on the bright dancing lake. He wrote a note as he stood, moving his pen deliberately and slowly across his pad. He stepped carefully across the room to look closely at prints hung on a wall, a framed copy of the Gettysburg Address. He penned a slow note.

When Gates rose the next time to change his seat, the reporter said, "I guess you're not really alone this whole week."

"What?" said Gates as he looked up at the man with surprise, disguising alarm.

"You've got these two with you," the reporter said as he gestured toward Rin and Amanda. "They look pretty comfortable here."

"Oh," said Gates. "I see what you mean. Yeah, they're getting along just fine. The pretty one belongs to my wife. She's a breeder. The other one is mine. He's with me almost all the time now."

The reporter tipped his head to hastily scratch down a note. Gates bowed back to his own reading, concealing the small jolt of satisfaction that surged through his thoughts.

Reginald Macklam knew the full schedule of the New York Times staff writer's observation day with Bill Gates. Not long after the five hours elapsed, leaving a comfortable period for the reporter to bid farewell, to settle into his car, to wend the long span of the arbored driveway and then roll off a safe distance on the public road that led him away, Macklam arrived at the lodge. He drove his own car. The awkward Chevrolet sport-utility that Debbie Green had piloted early that day remained at the hotel nearby, where both Macklam and Green had checked in yesterday. The drive back to the hotel was short enough for Amanda and Rin to share his back seat, he figured -- no need to engage the mammoth SUV for such a short jaunt. Macklam and Green planned to stay at the hotel another night. The reporter's access day ended too late for either of them to attempt the long drive back to headquarters this evening. Debbie Green was scheduled to leave the next morning, carting back Amanda in the huge Chevrolet. Macklam intended to stay at the hotel for another day or two. Earlier, Gates had told him to bring Rin to the lodge for long spells meant to reinforce the comfortable familiarity Rin had built with the chairman.

Inside the lodge, he found Gates speaking on the telephone about some dollars and cents concern that did not interest Macklam. He waited for Gates to finish.

"So how did your big day with the dogs go?" Macklam asked.

"He seemed like he was very impressed," Gates said.

"But I mean those two." Macklam wagged his head toward Rin and Amanda. "Did you do all right with them?"

"They were good," Gates responded. "In fact, it was even easier than I expected. Most of the time I forgot they were here. She must have a calming effect on him. He seemed quieter. He moved around a lot less than I'm used to."

"I'm not surprised," Macklam said, "but I'm very glad we all passed this first big test."

"We passed it with flying colors. In fact, I think there's a very good chance he'll get mentioned in the article when it comes out. We'll have to wait and see, but the guy definitely noticed him. He took a lot of notes and he seemed to be very interested in Rin over there. Amanda too. We'll have to wait and see, but I think I'll get described as a dog owner in the article. It'll get mentioned, at least."

"But was it subtle?" asked Macklam. "What I mean is, did it seem to be appropriate, did it seem to be natural having them here with you?"

"It seemed natural enough that I think they'll make it into the article," Gates told him.

"That's very nice, because of course that's what got us into this business in the first place. I mean, that's exactly the sort of results you've been hoping to have."

"I have to admit that I'm glad I stuck with it," said Gates. "At the beginning I didn't like the idea at all. It just didn't seem like it would be worth it. You already know that I was really ready to throw it in after that first big mess with that other one. What was his name?"

"Gandhi."

"Right. After that I never thought it would work. But now I have to admit that it wasn't all that much effort for the results we're starting to see. It hasn't been as hard as I thought. Rin fit in pretty easily and now it's working like Osborne first said: it's pointing straight toward the image we want."

"I think Gandhi could have brought us here too," said Macklam. "That first failure was our fault more than his and I'll take the fall for that. I should have handled him differently. With what we know now, if we brought Gandhi back here today he'd do every bit as well. Bring him back now and we could make him the star."

"Well, maybe" said Gates. "But Rin is the top dog now."

"I'll be bringing him by tomorrow, just like we scheduled," Macklam confirmed. "And the next day, too. Amanda here has to head back tomorrow, but Rin will be around."

"I have a couple of phone meetings scheduled," Gates mentioned. "So I'll be tied up with those for a while. But he shouldn't be in the way for that."

"No more so than he's been lately back at headquarters," said Macklam. "Rin's been doing very well with you."

"And the cook and the housekeeper will be back then, too," Gates added. "But they shouldn't have any trouble getting along with him."

"Everybody gets along with Rin," concluded Macklam. "Like you just said, he's the top dog."

The hotel was about twenty-five minutes by car, in the same, rough-hewn resort region as Caveat Lodge, but on a distant edge of the lake, far separated by shaggy, darkly treed and silent shoreline. When Macklam arrived at the hotel with Amanda and Rin, he parked in a distant corner of the lot, where the asphalt cut out a notch of forest. Macklam edged the car as far from the building entrance as he could squeeze it.

"There's some big open woods back here just begging for us to explore them," he said to Rin and Amanda. Rin climbed out of the rear door with eagerness, while Amanda followed more tentatively. "We'll let Debbie watch some more TV," Macklam said. "I doubt if she'll miss us if we head out for a while to see where this trail leads."

The trail started as an obscure gap in the understory that grew densely up to the edge of the parking lot. Rin brushed through rapidly, emerging in open forest that was floored more sparsely with low, rangy shrubs and ankle-high groundlings. With the low growth covering the ground more thinly inside, Rin saw out well ahead of himself, peering into the woods until too many of the towering trunks cut off his view. He stepped rapidly along the faintly worn path, pushed by anticipation and pulled by the subdued beauty of the undulating, overhung landscape that spanned ahead of him. He pulled up after Amanda lagged too far behind for him to comfortably speak to her. While waiting, he scanned contentedly among the columnar trunks and the burled stone croppings.

"Shouldn't we wait for Macklam?" Amanda asked him as she approached.

"He's okay," Rin answered. "He always lags behind me like this. He just likes to take his time. But don't worry: I always know exactly where he is. He'll let us know if he wants us to turn around or to turn in another direction or something. Right now we need to see where this trail will take us."

"It keeps going up this hill," she said.

"But the top's just ahead. We'll get a good look around when we get just up there."

Rin stopped at the crest of the rise and surveyed the open forest ahead of him.

"Let's stay this way," he said. "The trail follows the lake shore. We should find a place where it cuts in to the water."

They scampered a distance further. The path skirted a long, sloping bank, running parallel with the top edge of the incline.

"The water's down there," said Amanda. "If we go straight down I bet we'll reach the lake."

"I know," said Rin. "But look just ahead. It looks like the trees open up just up there. See how it's lighter? There must be a road or a clearing up there. Let's go see what it is."

The little trail brought them to the twin ruts of a lane. Instinctively Rin turned uphill, following the gladed road around a slow arcing bend to where it traced through a stone field and found the knobby crest of a knoll where the tree-cover thinned, growing sparse and admitting sunlight in porous abundance. Grass here grew gaily and tall. The afternoon sun still stood high, washing Amanda and Rin with rich light while they stood peering roundly at the earth that was crowned here.

After a moment Amanda said, "I'm sorry I didn't talk to you in the car when we drove up here last night."

"That's okay," answered Rin. "It was kind of late. I just figured you were tired."

"It was Dremmel," Amanda explained. "He told me I should keep my distance. That I shouldn't get too friendly with you."

"Which one is Dremmel?"

"He's the guy who always watches out for Debbie Green or Macklam to come. So he can make sure he's doing the right things."

"Oh, you mean the real nervous guy."

"Nervous?"

"Yeah. The guy who's always so jumpy. Who's always looking around at everything. He looks like he's scared of everything."

"Scared? I don't know if Dremmel is scared. He's real smart. He thinks about everything."

"Why did he say you should stay away from me?"

"I don't know. He just said it would be real bad if Bill Gates started thinking that I like you. If he started thinking you and I could get along together like we were just the same. He said it would be bad for all of us. He said I might lose the big home I live in. And those guys too. He said they might lose theirs. So I should do it for all of us, he said. Especially for those guys. I'd be doing them a big favor, he said. That's why I didn't talk to you at all. Because Dremmel said it would be a big favor to those guys. To all four of them. I really like those guys. They're all so nice to me. They all want to marry me. Every one of them: Georgie and Blake and even Web, and especially Dremmel. But I'm not ready for that. That's all I can tell them. But they're still real good friends. They all look out for me. Especially Dremmel. He tells me a lot of things. He's real smart and he's very well educated. He told me about Big Gandhi and how he's our leader but how he just disappeared. That's why Dremmel said I should ignore you. He wants to make sure we survive and don't follow Big Gandhi."

"Big Gandhi?" Rin wondered.

"Yeah. Don't you know about him?"

"No."

"Well, he's one of our breed. I guess that's why. Dremmel knows everything about him. Dremmel says only Bill Gates is above Big Gandhi. That's why he's not with us any more: because Bill Gates didn't like him. Dremmel knows everything about Bill Gates, too."

"But I've never seen Dremmel with Bill Gates," Rin said.

"He studies these things. He's real smart."

"Well, I wish he didn't tell you that you should stay away from me."

Amanda giggled. "Me too," she said.

With Rin she looked out around the open roundrel on which they stood, surveying the forest that walled all around the hill and peeking in at the openings where the lane that had led them here cut into the woods. The little road entered behind them and traced up the open knoll as a worn single footpath in the nodding grass, descending ahead of them to where the lane opened a second gap in the wall of the forest.

"We should go see where it leads," Rin said.

"What about Macklam?" Amanda asked him. "What if he doesn't come up here? What if he turns the other way and heads down by the water instead?"

"Oh, I think he'll come up here. I've walked with him long enough now to know that he'll head up the rise to see what he sees up here, just like us. He's not far behind us."

"It sure is beautiful up here," Amanda offered.

"It's beautiful because you're here."

She giggled. "Now you sound like Georgie," she said.

"No, I didn't mean it like that. I didn't mean it as a come-on line or anything. I meant that you make it beautiful by seeing it that way. It's something Ester told me. She said it's something you bring with you, not something you find when you get someplace. I mean, you have to be willing to see the beauty or it's just not there. You have to be able to see it. It's like, another person could just trudge through here and not see this place as anything special. But you see it as special because it's in you to see it that way. It's not just out there. The beauty's not something you find. It's something you make. That's kind of what I meant. Ester says it a lot better than I do."

"Is Ester the lady you live with?"

"Right."

"It sounds like you think a lot of her."

"She talks to me a lot. She tells me a lot of interesting things."

Amanda felt jealousy twinge.

"Is Ester your mother?" she ventured, disguising how eagerly she wondered about the woman's status with Rin. "One of my friends thought she might be your mother. Because of her age, I mean. She seems a little older than you. You know, like she's too old to be your girlfriend."

"She's a lot older than me," said Rin. "But she's not my mother. She's not my girlfriend either. I'd never met her till I moved in over there. She just takes care of the place."

"Oh, that's good," said Amanda, this time disguising relief. "I mean, it's good that you have someone who looks after things for you."

"It's nice because Ester is so nice. It's nice because she talks to me a lot. She tells me all sorts of things. She teaches me all sorts of things."

"Like what you just said about beauty? About putting beauty in a place instead of taking it out?"

"Right. Just like that. Except she says it better than I do. She says it so you understand exactly what she means. She didn't mean we're putting the beauty in this place. I think she'd say that this little hill with these woods all around it is beautiful all on its own. But our eyes have to be ready for it. We have to see it or it just won't be here for us. That's not quite right either. I just can't explain things the way she can. It's like, you have to have it already in you. You make things; you don't just find them. At least that's what Ester might say."

"It sounds like she and Dremmel should get together and talk. He's real smart too."

"Macklam's coming up the road now," said Rin. "He's not far behind us. Let's hurry back into the forest and follow this trail a little farther to see where it goes."

"Do you think we'll find another spot like this?" Amanda asked.

"Come on. Let's go see."

He stretched his legs into the descent, following the thin path downward through the grass toward the walled trees at the bottom of the knoll. Amanda bounced closely behind him. As they jounced down the sunwashed hill she said, "I wish I could stay here tomorrow with you."

"I wish you could too," Rin responded.

"Do you think you'll come back to this trail?"

"I don't know. Maybe not this same trail. But I'm sure I'll go someplace just as nice."

CHAPTER 8

Inside the cluttered offices of the Habitat Defenders Fund, Marci Waters sat down alone at a smeared table inside a closed and windowless meeting room in which the walls, acorn-colored with fake-wood paneling, rose bare and undifferentiated except for the door cut into one corner. She left the door open, expecting Justin Bainbridge to arrive some time soon. Well, she expected Justin Bainbridge to arrive. He might stomp in exceedingly late, she acknowledged. Even so, she felt sure he would make the meeting eventually. Bainbridge had asked to see her urgently. He wouldn't stand her up. At least not intentionally. There was always the chance that he would forget about the meeting entirely, she knew. But Justin Bainbridge loitered around the offices most every day anyway. Marci Waters had scheduled their meeting for the late morning because she knew this was the hour he would most reliably turn up in any event.

She carried in a bundle of files she had lifted from her desk. She could work as easily in here while she waited, she thought. From her chair Waters reached to tear off an arm's-length of brown towelette from a janitor's roll left standing on the table. She wadded it loosely and wiped a big arc of the table, clearing away crumbs and oily blots to clean a surface on which she could open a folder. From her stack she thumbed for the file containing a U.S. government grant application. She would complete all the forms for the government application first, she figured – not just because it demanded the most work from her, because the government grant forms were by far the most complex and confusing, the most voluminous, difficult, and, therefore, the most time consuming. But also, she felt eager to write for the government grant first because her effort would most likely pay off. The feds may demand more paperwork, but she knew that they gave up cash more easily than the big private groups. She would more likely get grant money from the government than from the Sierra Club, the World Wildlife Federation, or any of the other incorporated groups from which the Habitat Defenders Fund sometimes asked for support. She would get around to the private, incorporated groups for sure, because Marci Waters eagerly wanted all the dollars she could claim. Her organization's Campaign for Banalweck Shoals had pulled in so many small contributions from small private donors that now she had nearly enough money to pay for all of the planned restoration – and she would make sure it would be enough, because she would make sure that all of the contractors stuck to their price quotes and didn't exceed their original cost estimates. With nearly enough money for the project already in the bank, Waters now hoped to collect additional funds for the island restoration program, funds from grants like these. She planned to shift the extra money to the general operating budget of the Habitat Defenders Fund, to pay rent and utilities, to pay for travel and to support fund raising and what have you. She hoped to finish all the arcane government forms today, and maybe get started on a request to the Sierra Club, even if its outcome was less assured. But the moment she laid out the grant forms and determinedly took up her pen, Justin Bainbridge crashed in through the open door.

"Oh," said Marci Waters. "You startled me. I thought you'd be later."

"No way. Not today. They got me too pissed off this time," Bainbridge said. He crashed into a chair, slouched, then abruptly stretched forward to flip open a pizza box left lying near the center of the table. He flipped open a second box. He craned and surveyed the contents of both before he selected a slice from the first box he'd opened. He pulled off a bite before laying the pizza slice on the bare table where he sat.

"That's from last night," Marci Waters told him.

"I know. I was here when we got it."

"You know that you're supposed to pick up after yourself when you're still here after the cleaning crew leaves," she told him.

"Hey, I'm glad this is still here," Bainbridge answered. "I'm starving."

"What were you guys doing here so late last night?"

"We were talking about this. Talking about what's got me so pissed off right now. Talking about Microsoft." He chewed loudly on a second big bite of the pizza.

"About Microsoft?"

"Yeah. Well, you know: about Bill Gates. Bill Gates and Microsoft and his god dammed foundation. It's all the same thing. They all turned us down."

"We're only dealing with the foundation," said Marci.

"Okay, the foundation. The point is, the Bill and Melinda Gates Foundation, or whatever the fuck they call it, says it's not going to give us a grant we need for Ewell Sands. I can't tell you how much that pisses me off."

"But we already knew that might happen. I mean, we said it was a long shot when you said you were going to contact them to ask for the money. It's not their thing. It's not the kind of program they support. They're more into health. Into AIDS and malaria and all. We already said that."

"But they're like one of the only foundations with enough money to do this."

"But it's not what they do. We already said that."

"But it's what they *should* do," Bainbridge insisted. "What could be more important than this? We said that, too. We said that Ewell Sands is the biggest thing we're doing. It's our most important program. It's the future. It's where everything has to go."

"But it's longer term," said Marci Waters.

"But they got the money to do it right now. They could pay for the whole fucking thing. They could pay for it today. I don't care what else they're doing. They can keep doing all the AIDS and stuff if they want. They can do all that and still pay for Ewell Sands. Pay for all of it. Every penny. And why shouldn't they? What can be more important than this? We're going to take Ewell Sands and put it back exactly the way it was before any fuckin' person set a foot on it. *Exactly* the way it was."

"But it's so expensive."

"The Gateses have the money. They could do it right now."

"When did you get their rejection?"

"I got the letter yesterday. That's why I wanted to see you right away. Sorry I was so rude about it. But they've got me utterly pissed. I was sure they'd go for it, 'cause it's so goddamn vital. It's the future: re-genesis; erasing human impact. Instead all I got was a fucking form letter. Just like all the other turn-downs you get: 'we're sorry that we can't respond individually but due to the high volume of requests we get . . .' and all that bullshit. That got me pissed off more than anything – a form letter."

"But what can I do about it?" she asked him.

"We need to turn up the heat on them."

"What do you mean 'turn up the heat?'"

"I mean make 'em sweat. You know, make 'em see things our way."

"How do you propose to do that?" she asked him.

"I don't know. That's what I want to see you about."

"I don't know, Justin," she said. "I don't have any more ideas either. It's a really expensive project. Really expensive. We're not going to get that much money. At least not at the start. We already knew that. I guess the best thing to do right now is just make some more applications. You know, put in for some other grants. They won't pay for it all. Not by a long shot. But you might get enough to get it started."

"But Microsoft could pay for it all right now," he protested.

"Then wait a year and go ask them again. You know: wait for their next cycle to begin and then make another grant application. Just don't send it to Microsoft, okay? Make sure you send it to the Bill and Melinda Gates Foundation."

"Wait a whole year!" burst Bainbridge. "I can't wait a whole year. That's too goddamn long. We have to start right away. Right now. The longer we wait . . . you know, we've already waited too long. Ewell Sands is just getting farther and farther away from its pristine state. It just gets harder and harder to reconstruct it. It gets harder to do the modeling because the island just gets farther and farther away from its pristine, its pre-human state. We talked about all that. We said if we're going to wipe off all the traces of human impact and return it to its original, you know, to its pre-invasion state, we should start right away because first we have to model exactly what that pre-human condition looked like. That's even before any of the actual reconstruction can begin."

"But Justin, it's already been centuries . . . .."

"Exactly. That's why we can't wait any longer. This is the future. It's just a small start. This is the direction we need to go everywhere. To turn back human impact. Ewell Sands is just the start, to show that it can be done. It's a vital demonstration. It can't wait any longer."

"Okay, Justin. But I don't see what else can be done right now."

"We can make 'em sweat. That's what can be done. That's what I want to figure out: a way to make 'em sweat. A way to make 'em see things our way."

"How can you make them sweat?"

"I don't know. The usual way. Have protests and everything. Go there with signs and all that. Get the media involved."

"But what are you going to protest, Justin? These huge foundations turn down all sorts of requests. You have to understand how it works. We can't go there with signs and everything just because we're one in a million that they said no to. And you gotta be careful. Trust me: the Bill and Melinda Gates Foundation has a good reputation. A very good reputation. That's mostly because it's so big, of course. It spends all sorts of money, and then it spends even more money to make sure people know that it's spending money. Still, it's got a good reputation. You can't just go attacking them."

"I know. That's why I gotta get something on them. I gotta dig up some dirt."

"Justin, you're being ridiculous. Those guys are so big, they *are* charity. They *are* philanthropy. At least that's what everybody thinks. You aren't going to get any dirt on them."

"There's dirt on everybody. People dig things up all the time."

"What people?"

"People. You know. You see things all the time on the news. You read things on the internet. People are always digging up stuff on other people, no matter how good they look."

"Okay, there's investigative reporters. And then you've got those political guys that go after the people in the other party. But how are you going to do that?"

"That's the thing, you see. That's what we were talking about last night. You know Carl Eldad? His girlfriend works for the New York Times. I'm going to talk to her. She's not an investigative reporter or anything. She's a copy editor. That's her title. But she works on the business section."

"And?"

"They just did this big article about Bill Gates. Carl showed it to me. It talks about how he's a dog lover and how he has two dogs laying at his feet and everything."

"They wrote an article about that?"

"No, it's not about that. It's about something else. But they get into that in the article. They mention it. We figured, what the hell, if he's this big dog lover, you know, back to nature and everything, then he's really got to support Ewell Sands. It's as back to nature as you can get."

"So he's got a dog. What's that got to do with digging up dirt on him?"

"I don't know. You just gotta spin it right. You know, you gotta find a way to spin it."

"Spin what? That the guy has a dog?"

"Hell yes. You can spin anything. You know that. You just have to know how to do it."

"Okay, Justin, but I can't help you with this. I've got too many other things going on." She gestured toward the pile of file folders she had carried in from her office. "You'd be completely on your own with this."

"I already know that. I just wanted to let you know what I'm doing."

"And that goes for funding too," she told him. "I mean, I don't know how you expect to pay for this little dirt-digging expedition of yours. If it involves travel or if you're going to hire contractors, pay protesters or anything like that, there's no money for it. Things are already so tight. I can't budget anything for this."

"I know that, too. I'll cover this one on my own. Some other people too. That's what we talked about last night." He stretched upward to peer into the two pizza boxes flopped open upon the table. He selected a second piece. "I don't know why I'm so damn hungry today," he said.

As he chewed a large bite, Bainbridge spat, "When we were in here last night, Carl Eldad and me and the others decided to take this one on our own. To pay for it ourselves. The only thing we'll need from you is the forms. You know, the charitable contribution forms we need to fill out, whatever you call them, so we can deduct it all from our taxes. So we'll pay for it. We've really had enough, you know. I mean, it would be insane to wait any longer. We're gonna dig up something. Any travel, any expenses, anything, we'll pay for it on our own. But we got to do something right now to make them see this our way. It's so fuckin' urgent. When they finally see that, there won't be any problems. As soon as we can get their attention and make them wake up, they'll see how vital this is and there won't be any problems at all. They'll fund us right away. How could they not? They can still do all their other things if they want. I don't care. But they can afford to fund this completely and they will. I'm sure of it. They'll understand that we have to start this re-genesis thing right away. We have to put things back the way they were before people fucked them up. Just look at all the species that have gone extinct already. We can't have any more. We can't wait at all. We can't compromise. Those people have to change their thinking now. Right now!"

CHAPTER 9

Reginald Macklam walked into the small office inside the kennel building and almost winced at the sight of the walls that were now newly painted. He disliked blue. Macklam flinched when he inhaled the soapy odor from the curing paint.

"I guess we're not going to want to stay in here for our meeting," he said to Debbie Green, who sat waiting at the desk of drab gray metal. A laptop computer stood opened in front of her.

"The smell's not too bad," she said. "Not after you get used to it. I always kind of liked this new-paint smell anyway."

"I don't like it," said Macklam. "I don't really care for the color blue, either."

"But your eyes are blue," said Green."

"But I can't see my own eyes, now can I?" Macklam quipped.

Green snickered.

"I don't mind some of them," said Macklam. "But this particular blue here looks like the inside of a swimming pool. I wonder who picked it out."

"I did."

"My God, Debbie, you could have asked me first."

"There wasn't any time. The painters were here and they were ready to start. They had some different colors in their van and I had to pick one of them right away."

"The painters told you what color you had to use?"

"Well, kind of. I mean, they didn't say I had to use this color. They had about five or six different colors I could pick from. But it had to be one of those. They said the contract called for one of their, their . . . oh, what did they call them?"

"One of their *awful* colors?"

"No. Not that. They said the contract called for one of their standard colors, or something like that. There was five or six of them. They had the gallons right there in their van."

"I guess they're efficient at least," said Macklam. "Come on. Let's sit out there in your work area and talk about this stuff out there."

"What if I open the window?"

"That's a really good idea. Open it as far as it goes. But let's still sit out there."

Debbie Green snapped shut the laptop as she rose.

"Wait a minute," said Macklam. "What are you doing there? Were you using that? What were you doing on the computer just now? Don't tell me you're finally starting to enter your own daily assessment forms?"

"This? No," she said. "I'm still doing those by hand on the pages you printed out for me. I've got lots of those left. This here is just for e-mail."

"E-mail," blurted Macklam. "When did you start doing e-mail?"

"I don't know. I've done it pretty much forever. Or at least for as long as e-mail has been around."

"But you told me you hated computers. You told me you quit your last job because they made you use one. You said you wouldn't use one here.

That's why I printed out all those forms for you: so you wouldn't have to use a computer. Now you tell me you use one for e-mail?"

"But that's for work," she tried to distinguish. "That's different from e-mail. I just don't like all the typing and all the stuff they make you do for work."

"There's no difference," Macklam exclaimed. "You type stuff in, you move the cursor, you click around to different places. I bet you type more to write your e-mails than you would to fill in one of these forms. But no, you have me doing that for you. Every day. You have me type them in after you fill them out by hand. I don't believe it. I'm sure it's a lot harder for you to write with a pen on these forms than it would be for you to just type it in on the screen. And then I have to type it in for you anyway. It doesn't make any sense."

"I just hate the way you have to type in everything just right. Everything has to be exactly perfect or it just won't take it. You know: if you spell a name wrong or something you get one of those little signs that pop up in the middle of your screen, one of those *data entry error* or *improper code* thingies. Then you have to go back and fix it."

"That doesn't make any sense," said Macklam.

"Yes it does. For some things it does. For some things, like, what if you want to write something in a record, add something to an official record. If you want to get to that record before you can add anything, first you have to type in its name just right, spelled perfectly and everything, or the computer just won't take it. You get one of those little sign thingies that says you made a mistake."

"No you don't. Not here you don't. I don't know what kind of computer system you've used in the past, but here it's all set up for you. All you do is move the cursor and click and it's all right there. You don't type in any names. Sure, you have to type in your notes when you're filling out the daily assessment sheets. But you can spell things any way you want to there. It'll reflect on you, that's all. But the computer will still take it, no matter what you write."

"It just takes so long to do everything," she said.

"I don't care how long it takes you. You're going to start doing it yourself from now on. I can't believe I've been doing it for you and it turns out you're using the computer anyway. It turns out you're sending e-mails. Who do you send them to, anyway?"

"I don't know. To a lot of people. To my friends. And my mother. I send a lot to my mother."

"Well tell mom I said hello. But not until you fill out the assessment sheets every day. Using this here computer. Four of them, right? That's one for Dremmel, Blake, Web and Georgie. One each. You do that every day before you read your e-mails. Do you understand?"

"Okay."

"And I don't want you to quit on me like you did your last job, just because you have to use a computer. If you can use it for fun, you can use it here, too."

"I'm not going to quit," she said. "I like this job."

"That's good," said Macklam. "To tell you the truth, I like it too. But I'll tell you, sometimes I wonder if I'm going to get lazy, because it seems like this job is a little too easy. But let's get to it now, before I pass out from these fumes. Open that window like you said and let's sit out here in the work area to go over this stuff while this room airs out. Open it all the way so it airs out fast."

The work area was the section of the building behind the indoor quarters of Amanda, Ester and Rin, and the four toffs. The back wall of their bedrooms, the partition wall that reached just three-quarters of the way to the ceiling, ran the full length of the work room where Debbie Green stored food and supplies, where she kept all the cleaning equipment and the leashes and the crates used for traveling. In the work room she bathed the dogs. She meted out their food twice a day and washed out their dishes and bowls.

"You have to start keeping this place picked up," said Macklam as they settled onto stools at a stainless counter top. "We talked about that before. It's a lot easier to work if you don't have all this stuff left out all over the place."

"I know," she said. "I was working on it."

"Okay, that's good. Just please keep working on it. Maybe next time we'll have more room if this counter here is cleaned off. But, now, for today, here's the deal," Macklam began. "What the missus wants from us is some kind of an interim report. I don't know why, exactly, because she's been getting a daily report with these assessment sheets we were just talking about. I mean, I thought that was the point of all those, and why should we have to do an interim assessment today when we've been doing it all along, when we've been doing it every day on the assessment sheets? I doubt if she's even looked at them, that's why. I doubt if she's even looked at the summary or the tabulation or whatever it is the computer is supposed to do with those forms as we enter them. I almost wonder if she's losing interest. I've seen that happen before with wealthy people. They get an idea and it sounds great at the time but then they lose interest in it. Or they just get caught up in other things. I don't know if that's what's happening here but it seems kind of odd to me that she wants this interim report when we've been giving her assessments all along. We're supposed to keep doing those, too, by the way, so I don't know why she has us doing this. I think sometimes a person lets things slip and then all the sudden they remember and feel guilty or whatever so they say, I've got to get back on track with that. I've got to get caught up or whatever. So they get in a flutter and come up with something new to do to fix the fact that they haven't been paying attention. But it's all in a rush so they don't really think it through. Like this report. It only means duplicated work for us. I don't think she's thought it through at all because she already has all the information. But, well, whatever. This shouldn't be too bad so instead of jawboning about it I guess we just need to get it done. I need just a quick assessment from you covering each of those four fellows out there. Then I'll write up a paragraph or two on each for our interim report. I think that should give Mrs. Gates what she's looking for. So let's start at the top. What do you see in Georgie so far?"

"Georgie? He's really cute. I think he's the best looking guy out there."

"That may be," said Macklam, "but remember, we're supposed to be evaluating them for intelligence and temperament and behavior. They're all good looking, but the missus wants to know which one is the best acting."

"Right. But I think Georgie is real smart, too."

"Okay. But why? I need a lot more than that. This has to come mostly from you because you spend a lot more time with those four than I do. It turns out that I'm away with Rin a lot more than we ever expected. I mean, at the start of all this I didn't think Gates would stick with it like he has. I didn't expect him to keep Rin around him almost all of the time. I recommended it, I know that, but I just didn't expect him to do it. Not the way his attitude was at the start. But it turns out that he's doing very well. I've got to give him credit for that. I guess he's really serious about changing his image. I guess he really listens to those people he's hired – those image consultants who came up with the idea in the first place. So I'm up there with him and with Rin a lot more than we ever thought. That means this report has to come mostly from you."

"But I didn't think I'd be evaluating them or anything," complained Green.

"You've been evaluating them from the start," countered Macklam. "That's the point of the daily assessments, right? The ones you're now going to do on the computer."

"Yeah, but now you're saying you want more. You're saying I have to tell you what's going on so you can write this report. Like it's all from me. What about the rest of them? I thought Mrs. Gates was going to come down here and evaluate them too. She was going to have some others come, too, I thought. Now you're making it sound like it's all on my shoulders."

"Well, you're right about that," said Macklam. "The missus said she was going to do the heavy lifting, she was going to do most of the evaluation and the choosing and all. Our forms were just supposed to, you know, give her a little more input. But, well, that's not the way it's working out. But whatever's going on, like I said, we need to do this now. I need to get this interim report to her so I need to know what you think about each of those fellows. Now you think Georgie is cute, which is fine but irrelevant. But you also think he's very bright. You can start by telling me why you think that."

"He's so independent," she said. "He likes to be alone because he's not always with the others. Let's just say he doesn't follow the crowd. He thinks for himself. That's why I think he's real smart."

"But how do you know what he's thinking about?" Macklam asked her.

"I don't know. You can just kind of tell that he's not interested in what all the others are interested in. That's why he's not with them as much."

"I don't know," mused Macklam. "If I had to guess what he was thinking about, I'd figure he's only thinking about himself. But you've certainly seen more of him than me, so I'll take note of that. Who's next on your list?"

"Next I like Web," she said. "He's the strong, silent type. He's very good mannered, too. I mean, he never gives me any kind of trouble. He just does exactly what I want him to do, all the time. I think Web is smart, just like Georgie. I think he's one of the alphas. You know, one of the leaders.

Georgie is too. I think Georgie and Web are the two leaders. But especially Web. It's like the others want to be with him. I see Dremmel with him all the time. It's like Dremmel wants to learn things from Web. I see Georgie with him too. It's like they all look up to Web, because they always want to be with him."

"But you said Georgie is alone all the time."

"Well not *all* the time. Georgie is alone a lot of the time. That's why I say he's so independent. But when he's together with one of the others it seems like it's always with Web. At least most of the time it's with Web."

"And Dremmel too?" asked Macklam. "I mean, you think Dremmel follows Web like Georgie does?"

"I think Dremmel follows him more," said Green. "It's like Dremmel is always with Web. But some of that might just be because Dremmel is real friendly. I really like Dremmel. He's real sweet and affectionate. At first he was pretty shy. I mean, he always hung back and he looked unsure about everything. I think it was because everything was so new. But now he always comes up to see me and he always stays right beside me. Sometimes I even have to push him away from me just so I can get something done. He's real sweet like that. Like he really wants me to know how much he likes me."

"Really?" said Macklam. "Because I took Dremmel to be the nervous type. The jumpy type. Like he's always afraid someone or something is going to give him a swat."

"I did too, at first. But now he's really, really sweet to me. I mean, he cuddles right next to me all the time. Maybe he's with Web so much just because he's so friendly."

"So you think Dremmel and Georgie follow Web. So Web is our leader out there?"

"Yeah. Well, he's one of them. Like I said, it's Georgie and Web together that the others look up to. But, yeah, I guess mostly it's Web. Georgie's more, like I said, more independent."

"Where does all this leave Blake?" Macklam asked.

"Blake? Oh, yeah. I forgot about Blake. He doesn't impress me too much. I mean, he's always just goofing around. Every time I see him he's running or jumping or doing something like that. He's not real smart, I don't think."

"He's too active?"

"Well, not too active. But all he ever wants to do is race around and play."

"Doesn't he get along with the others?"

"Well, I don't know. I guess he does. He's with Amanda a lot, I guess."

"So he's not anti-social?"

"No, I wouldn't say he's anti-social. He's just not real smart. I guess that's what it is."

"Well, anyway," said Macklam, "it seems safe to say that he's not a leader. Is that right?"

"Yeah, I'd say he's definitely not like Georgie and Web. He's not smart like them."

"Okay," said Macklam. "I think we have enough here now. I don't know exactly what Mrs. Gates is looking for, but this should at least make us look like we're on the ball. I'll give her a quick write-up on each one of those guys in there. Not that it will do her any good if she doesn't get down her and take charge of this thing like she said she was. This sure hasn't worked out the way I thought it would. Not so far, anyway. Like I was just saying, I thought Bill Gates was the one who would let things slip. He just didn't seem committed. But now it turns out that he's very committed. He said that himself and from everything I've seen now, I believe him. It turns out he's spending more time with Rin than I ever expected. If I didn't know better,

I'd say he's even getting to like our friend Rin. I was telling him the other day that it's too bad he didn't try this hard with Gandhi. I mean, Gandhi was great, too. Bill just didn't take the time to see it. I told him, bring Gandhi back and you'll see exactly the same results. Not to take anything away from Rin. But Gandhi could be Bill's dog now, if he was back here. I think Bill would see that now. Now that he's tried so hard with Rin, he'd see how much Gandhi has to offer after he brought him back."

"And Gandhi had breeding," noted Debbie Green. "He was an Aussie through and through."

"That's right," said Macklam. "I guess that's the irony. If Gandhi was here, he'd be the perfect mate for Amanda out there."

CHAPTER 10

While Green and Macklam conversed, the others slept unaware on their side of the partitioning wall. Except for Georgie. Georgie had remained awake, watching eagerly for the sun to arc a short distance beyond its zenith, waiting for the air to fully saturate with warmth. When that time arrived, he felt assured that the others would rest until the day's heat diminished. Georgie paced cautiously through the hallway that led outside. He glanced sidelong into each of the bedrooms as he passed them, noting that Web, Blake and Dremmel remained settled contentedly inside the air-conditioned building. Before going out, Georgie doubled back quietly to Web's room. He lingered in the doorway, watching impatiently for Web to glance up and notice him. Georgie shifted and sighed as loudly as he dared. At last Web lifted his head. After Web started to rise, Georgie turned to lead him quietly down the hallway to the outside door. Once he was out of their house, Georgie trotted eagerly across the whole yard, stopping at the far outer boundary where the over-arching tree threw so much welcoming shade. He looked back to make sure that Web was following. He waited until Web was fully beside him before he spoke, keeping his tone quiet, yet trying to maintain a casual, ordinary voice.

"Those other guys aren't following you, are they?" he asked Web.

"No, Georgie. I didn't see 'em, anyway. It looked to me like they were just lying down. Like they were sleeping. I only came out here because I saw you coming out. You don't usually come out here now. 'Specially not this time of day. I just kind of wondered what's up."

"I'll tell you what's up," lathered Georgie. "I figured out how to sneak out of here. I'll need your help for sure. That's what I wanted to talk to you about. I tried it alone but it just doesn't work. But if you'll help me I know I can make it. I can get over that wall into Debbie Green's room and once I'm in there I can get to Amanda's place. I can go wherever I want. I'm sure I can. I just need to get over that wall and now I know a way I can do it."

"But do you think that might get us in trouble?" said Web.

"No it won't get us in trouble," replied Georgie emphatically. "Nobody's going to know about it. Nobody's going to find out. Not anybody. I'm going to sneak out and get back before anyone knows. But you gotta help me. The only way I'll get out is with your help. You'll do that for me, Web, won't you? You told me before that you'd help me get out."

"Well, yeah, Georgie. I'm not sayin' I won't help. I'm just kind of wondering, you know, if getting out is such a good idea. I mean, what if you got caught or something? That could cause a whole lot of trouble."

"I'm not getting caught," stressed Georgie. "Come on, Web. You know me. You know I'll be able to do this. Heck, you and me, we've done all kinds of things together. You know what I can do. I can do this with you. Together. With just a little bit of help. Listen, Web, this is all you have to do. You know Debbie Green? You know how she comes in to clean once in a while with that big shop-vac, that big canister vacuum with a hose? You know how it's on wheels and everything? You've seen how she never finishes it, right? Not all right away, I mean. She'll do this room and that room and then maybe roll the big vac into the next room but then maybe she'll leave it for a while.

Sometimes she leaves it overnight and comes back the next day to finish. You've seen all that, right? She just pushes it into a corner and leaves it there till she gets back the next day to finish. And sometimes she even leaves it there for two nights. Right? You've seen all that, right?"

"Yeah, Georgie. I've seen it. Everybody's seen it. Sometimes she leaves it in my room too."

"She leaves it all over the place. And it's just the right height. If I take a couple of steps and jump up onto it, I can spring myself over the wall. I know I can. But here's the problem: those wheels. I tried it once. I thought I could do it without your help. I mean, I didn't want to bother you, because I knew you'd be concerned. Concerned about my safety, I mean. Just like you are right now. But those wheels, they make it slide when I jump on it. It slides and kind of tips so I can't spring up over the wall. But if you help me, we can push it tight against the wall and then you can hold it there. You can just lean your body against it real hard and hold it there so it doesn't roll when I jump on it. Then I can spring up to the top for sure and get over that back wall. I'll drop down into Debbie Green's room and from there I can go wherever I want."

"But what if we all end up getting in trouble?"

"Nobody's going to get in trouble, Web. I already told you that. No one's gonna even know. Just you and me. We'll be the only ones who know about it. And Amanda too, I mean. But like I told you before, it'll be a surprise to her."

"But what if something goes wrong?"

"Nothing's going to go wrong. Come on, Web. You know me. We're good friends. At least I thought we were. But man, I gotta tell ya, now you're starting to sound like Dremmel. Like all the sudden you're scared of every little thing."

"Dremmel just likes to figure things out," said Web. "He wants to know what he's getting into and all that stuff. Dremmel always figures out what's going to happen next."

"I know. But this is one thing that I'm sure can't go wrong. I'm sure of it. Absolutely certain. And, hey," said Georgie, "what about Amanda? Just think about her for a second. She's over there all alone all the time. I mean, we talk to her a lot outside in the yard and everything, but no one ever visits her. No one ever goes over there and just sits down with her for a while to visit or anything. She's gotta be lonely, don't you think? I mean, it's different for us because we're all together all the time. Like you and me and all the things we do together all the time. But it's not like that for Amanda, is it? I mean, don't you think she'd like to have someone over at her place for once? That's why I wanna get over there. So Amanda doesn't feel so lonely all the time. I won't have to stay long. I mean, I won't stay long at all. I'll barely be gone at all. That's how I know I won't get caught. I'll be real fast – out and back in right away, in almost no time at all. I'll just surprise Amanda, make her laugh and feel happy. It'll be great, don't you think? I'll just step in and say hi and I'll only stay for a real short time before I'm back in here. Nobody will know except you and me and Amanda. It'll be great. But I can't do it unless you help me, Web."

"You'd really just be gone for a minute?" Web asked.

"Well, yeah. Of course. I mean, maybe more than just one minute. I mean, what can you do in a minute? But it will be real fast. I won't be gone long at all. And then I'll come right back in and no one will ever know."

"'Cause I'll be waiting there up against that vacuum cleaner," said Web. "I mean, I can't be standing there holding that thing for a long time while I'm waiting for you to come back. Someone will notice me for sure."

"No," sang Georgie. "You won't have to wait at all. That's the beauty of it, Web. I guess I should of told you that already. No wonder you were so worried. But you don't have to wait at all. See, I've been watching the door. I watch the door for when Debbie Green comes in and out because for a while I thought that would be the way to go. I thought I could figure out some way to get out through the door. But on the inside here, on our side, it's made so we can't turn that little knob they use. Only Debbie Green or Reginald Macklam or somebody like them can turn that to get out of here. But on the other side, on their side, there's just a handle you push down. I've seen it when they come in. I can just push down that handle and push the door open and come back in any time I want. It's great. Once I get out, once you help me get out, I can come back in whenever I want. I can sneak back in and no one will ever know I was gone."

"But you'd come back in right away, right?" asked Web.

"Of course I would. I already told you that. It's just a quick visit to cheer up Amanda and make her feel good. Then I'll be right back in here. You can just hold the vacuum steady for me for a second so I can get out over that wall. Then you'll just go away and forget about it and I'll be right back in before you know it. You'll do that for me, won't ya, Web?"

"You can't ever tell anyone about it, either," Web bargained. "I mean, Dremmel might get pretty mad if he found out. Especially if he found out I helped you and everything."

"Of course I won't tell," said Georgie. "And I'll make sure Amanda doesn't say anything either. I mean, I'll tell her it has to be a secret. She'll do that for us, Web. No one will ever find out."

"When do you want to do it?" asked Web. "Do you want to do it tonight?"

"No, Web. I can't do it tonight. How could I do it tonight? I just told ya, I have to wait for Debbie Green to leave the vacuum in just the right place. In my room our yours. Then I have to make sure no one else is around. I have to make sure that Dremmel and Blake are sound asleep, or that they aren't somewhere where they're gonna hear me. I can't let them find out I'm sneaking over there to Amanda's. So everything's gotta be just right and I don't know when that will be. I just have to watch for it and then make my move. We'll only have a little bit of time. That's why I wanted to talk to you now. I wanted to explain the whole thing to you now and make sure you're ready to help me. Now I'll just watch for it, Web. When Debbie Green leaves that vacuum in just the right spot and when we've got a minute alone from Dremmel and Blake, I'll give you a sign and we can sneak over and do it. You'll help me, wont' ya, Web? You'll do that for me, right?"

"If you promise you'll just be gone for just a really short time."

"Of course, Web. I already told you that. That's the whole plan. But you can't give it away. You can't say a word to anybody. Not even a slip. Make sure of that, Web, or I'll really get mad. We gotta shut up now, 'cause here comes Dremmel, damn it. Now don't say a word, Web. Make sure of it. If he asks what we're doing right now, tell him we're just resting. Tell him we're just resting here and talking about how hot it is today."

But Dremmel showed no concern about Georgie and Web and their fast conversation. Instead he accosted them with news that he couldn't contain, rushing out words as he approached them on the pad of comforting shade. He had overheard the discussion between Macklam and Green, at least bits of it.

"You guys should have been inside," Dremmel said. "I can't believe what I just heard. From Debbie Green and Macklam. They were talking and I heard them. They're bringing back Big Gandhi."

"Big Gandhi," repeated Web. "Really? Back here?"

"Bringing him back when?" asked Georgie with a slant of suspicion.

"I don't know when," Dremmel answered. "They didn't say. They just said he's coming back."

"I can't believe I'll finally get to meet him," said Web.

"Are you sure about that?" Georgie asked Dremmel.

"I heard it with my own ears. Blake heard it too. He came in my room and woke me up 'cause he heard them talking first. Blake must know more. He heard them for longer than I did. He heard them while I was still napping. By the time he woke me up I just caught the end."

"Then where is he now?" queried Georgie.

"He's still inside. I told him to stay in for a while and listen, in case they come back. I think they were done but just in case they come back and say more I don't want to miss it."

"But here he comes now," Georgie gently sneered.

"Where?" Dremmel said as he turned around to look at the door to their house. Blake was padding quickly toward them.

"I told you to stay inside," Dremmel called at him.

"I did stay inside," Blake shot back. "I stayed in long enough. They're not going to say anything else. I heard them both go out. I heard the door open and close and now there's nobody in there. If you don't believe me you can go inside yourself."

"Okay," said Dremmel. "I just didn't want to miss anything."

"Then you should of stayed inside yourself."

"Okay."

"What else did you hear them say?" Web asked eagerly.

"They didn't say anything else," Blake repeated. "I just told you, they both just left."

"No," Dremmel corrected. "He means, what did you hear that I didn't hear. I told them Big Gandhi is coming back, but that's almost all that I heard because you woke me up near the end. I told them you must have heard more, because you were listening for longer."

"There's not too much more than just that," Blake said, seeming sullenly defensive. "Before that they were talking a little bit about us. But not too much. I didn't hear too much of that. I didn't start paying attention till near the end."

"What did they say about us?" Web asked eagerly.

"I don't know. I just said, I didn't really hear it. I didn't pay any attention. When I heard them they were talking about Dremmel. That's why I went to wake him. I wanted him to hear it too. Macklam said Dremmel's too afraid of everything. He said Dremmel's too shaky. That's the honest truth. That's exactly what I heard him say so don't get mad at me. I'm just telling you what Macklam said and that's why I went to wake you up. But by the time I did they were talking about other stuff. They started talking about Big Gandhi. That's the part you heard, Dremmel."

"But I didn't hear all of it," Dremmel responded. "I didn't hear them say a word about me. I only heard the part at the end when they were talking about Big Gandhi. You didn't tell me they were talking about me."

"I didn't have a chance to," said Blake. "By the time you woke up they were on to Big Gandhi and so we just tuned in to that. Then you got all excited and trotted out here before I had a chance to tell you what else they were saying."

"Quit arguing about it," Georgie cut in. "Everybody already knows that Dremmel is jumpy and shaky and everything, so who cares. But what about Big Gandhi? That's what I want to know. What did you guys hear about Big Gandhi?"

"I told you," said Dremmel, "I only heard the end of it. I heard them say that Big Gandhi has breeding. Then they said he's the perfect match for Amanda. I never heard them say anything bad about me."

"What?" gaped Georgie. "They said they're bringing him back for Amanda?"

"They said Big Gandhi has breeding, and he's perfect for Amanda."

"But I have breeding too," Georgie protested.

"So do I," said Blake. "I've got just as much as anyone."

"But when is he coming?" Georgie asked.

"Yeah, Blake," said Dremmel. "Since you think you heard so much, when did they say he's coming back here?"

"I don't know," said Blake. "I didn't get that. I don't think they ever said exactly when he's coming back."

"Do you think it will be soon?" asked Web.

"I said I don't know."

"Then tell us exactly what you do know," Georgie demanded. "Tell us what you heard."

"I heard them say that Bill Gates spent so much time with that nonnie Rin that now he wants Big Gandhi back. Macklam said they can bring him back because he has so much to offer everybody. They said he has breeding and everything. That's the part Dremmel heard. And he heard 'em say that Big Gandhi is just right for Amanda."

"When do you think he'll be here, Dremmel?" Web asked.

"I don't know either. Blake's right: they never said when. We never heard anything about when. But they said he's coming back. That's unbelievable. It's not the end. I mean, everyplace else we've been, we've always seen everybody just disappear, just vanish sooner or later and never come back. And never a word in advance. Never a word about where they were going or why. Just gone. But now Big Gandhi is coming back. That's incredible. He's the only one. Because he has breeding. Like us. I wish they'd have said when. I can't wait to meet him. I can't wait to see what he's like."

"I can't either," said Web.

"All we need to do now is hold on. You know, hold on till Big Gandhi gets back," said Dremmel. "We're like him. We all have breeding too. If Big

Gandhi can come back, I mean, if he doesn't have to go away and vanish, then all we have to do is be like him. We need to see what he's like and what he does and then we'll be safe here too."

"Hey," Web exclaimed, "I see what you mean. We can follow Big Gandhi and then we'll be safe."

"That's right" said Dremmel. "After all, it's Bill Gates himself who's bringing him back. I heard that myself. Blake heard it too. All we need to do now is hang on till he gets here so we can see what he's like. So he can teach us to be just like him."

"That fixes everything," cheered Web. "For everybody."

"But while we're waiting we can't do anything that's going to get us in trouble. None of us can and I really mean that," Dremmel warned. "The last thing we need is to have something happen before Big Gandhi returns. If we sit tight, we'll be okay. But if somebody goes and does something they're not supposed to do, anything, something that gets Bill Gates mad or even Macklam or Debbie Green mad, then that could cause problems for all of us. We're all here together remember, and Big Gandhi can't help any of us if something happens to us before he gets here. Georgie and Blake, you guys can get a little too risky sometimes. You have to realize now that there's too much at stake. You can't do anything you're not supposed to do, anything that might get us in trouble."

"I'm not gonna do anything," griped Blake. "What could I do that's so bad anyway? We're always just in here all the time."

"That's one thing you can do," said Dremmel. "You need to make sure you stay in here. I saw you trying to jump out over the fence before. You were standing right over there and trying to jump over to Amanda's."

"I never tried to jump out of here," countered Blake.

"You just have to make sure you never do," Dremmel warned. "That's got to be the worst thing you could do now, because now we're so close. Now we know it's going to be okay, now that Big Gandhi is coming back here to teach us how he did it. All we have to do is hold on till he gets here. You understand that, right Blake? And you too Georgie, right? I mean, Georgie, you can't go doing anything either. Right? You've got to be good too, right?"

"Hey, I'll be good," answered Georgie. "I'm always good."

"We need to tell Amanda, too," Dremmel said. "She's like us. She's got breeding like we do, so this affects her as much as it affects us. It means she's safe too, no matter what."

"I'll tell her," said Blake. "I talk to her all the time anyway."

"Yeah, but that's just small talk," Dremmel said. "This time this is something that's really important. I think I better be the one who tells her about this."

"It's not all just small talk," Blake sharply rebutted. "We talk about a lot of serious stuff, too. Just because it's not the kind of stuff you like to talk about – who wants to talk about the kind of stuff you talk about anyway?"

"Well this news about Big Gandhi is the kind of stuff that everybody wants to talk about," Dremmel retorted. "This is stuff that everyone *needs* to talk about. That's why I have to tell Amanda. It's too important to forget any part of it, to leave any parts out. I have to make sure she understands everything, that she has the whole story."

"But I'm the one who heard the whole story," Blake blurted. "You just said yourself that you only heard the very end of what they said."

"I mean the whole story about what this means," Dremmel elaborated. "Heck, anyone can tell her what you just heard, and from what you just told us, you didn't hear a whole lot more than I did anyway. But I'm the one who figured out what it all means to us. That's the part she needs to know. She needs to know how important this is."

"I can tell her all that just as good as you can," Blake insisted.

"No. You…" Dremmel began.

"Oh, would you two just shut up and knock it off," interrupted Georgie. "Who cares who tells her? Let's just let Web tell her. That will settle this once and for all."

"Okay," Web said. "I'll tell her if you think I should, Georgie."

"Yeah, I think you should, just so these two don't stand here and argue about it all day. Don't you guys have anything better to do? Why don't you go back inside and listen some more. Maybe Debbie Green and Macklam will come back and have more to say. If this is so important, shouldn't you be listening for that? Maybe they'll even tell you when Big Gandhi is going to come back."

"That's true," said Dremmel. "There's more we need to find out. This is already so amazing. Big Gandhi is coming back! It would be incredible if we found out exactly when. I wouldn't have to worry so much about you guys if I knew exactly when he would get here. Hey, for once Georgie's right – ha! We should go inside and listen because maybe there'll be more. I mean, maybe they just stepped out. Maybe Debbie Green and Macklam will come right back and start talking again. We can't miss that. Let's go inside and see if we can find out anything else about Big Gandhi's return."

Dremmel led the way, scooting eagerly back toward their home in the subdivided building. Web scooted eagerly right behind him.

"I get to hear it too," said Blake indignantly pouting. "I'm the one who heard everything the first time. I get to know what comes next." He fell in line behind Dremmel and Web, hunching his shoulders in brooding protest as he trod more slowly and subdued.

Georgie hung back entirely. He waited until the other three were well on their way before he called out, "hey Web. Web. Hold on a second. There's one more thing I wanna ask ya."

Dremmel continued toward the building with his anticipation uninterrupted. Blake only glanced back at Georgie, but kept to his glowering pace. Georgie waited until both of them disappeared through the door inside, until Web had fully arrived at their meeting spot in the shade, before he began with his voice lowered again.

"Sorry, Web," he said, "but I just had to see you right now. This is even more important than it was before. It's more important that I get out now. As soon as I can. I'm just tellin' ya that now so you're ready. It's gonna happen real soon, just as soon as I can, so you hafta be ready."

"But wait a minute, Georgie," said Web. "You heard what Dremmel just said. He said we can't do anything now that's bad. Anything that, you know, breaks the rules. It's all different now, now that Big Gandhi is coming back."

"I know it's all different. That's the point. That's why I gotta get over there right away to see Amanda. You heard what they said. They said he's the perfect mate for Amanda. There's no way I'm gonna wait around for him to show up. I'm gonna get over there right away."

"But Georgie…"

"Come on, Web. You can't go backin' out now. You already said you would help me. You said that right here just a little while ago. So what about Dremmel. There's nothing different about that. Hell, even Debbie Green and Macklam said he's afraid of everything. You heard Blake tell us that just now. We already knew from before that he doesn't want anything like this going on. Well who cares? It's all just the same as before. I'll be out real quick and I'll get back before anyone knows I was gone. Just like we said a little while ago. Come on, Web. You're my best friend. You're the one guy I can count on to help me."

"But Dremmel just said…"

"Who cares what Dremmel just said. Even Debbie Green and Macklam think Dremmel's too jumpy and scared. We both heard Blake just say that. Besides, I'll be back here right away and Dremmel will never find out."

"You're sure you'd be back real fast?"

"Yes, Web. I already said that. You know you can count on me, same as I count on you. But it's gotta be soon. I want you to be ready because now with Big Gandhi, I gotta get over there just as soon as I can. I'll come get you the first chance I get."

"And then you'll come right back?"

"Yes, Web, I'll come right back. Hey, and don't say anything to Amanda about this. Remember? It has to be a surprise. You gotta remember that. Especially now that you're gonna be tellin' her what they heard about Big Gandhi and everything. When you talk to her you can't say a word about me comin' over. You'll remember, right?"

"I'll remember, Georgie."

"You promise you won't say a word?"

"Don't worry, Georgie. I promise."

CHAPTER 11

Web approached his assignment diligently, remaining outside in the yard and watching for Amanda almost from the moment his conversation with Georgie had ended. When eventually Amanda stepped out of her house, Web sidled anxiously close to her and announced that Dremmel and the others had picked him to tell her the important news that Big Gandhi was soon coming back. They didn't know when, Web said, but Dremmel was trying right now to find out the exact time of Big Gandhi's return. What they knew for certain so far, Web explained to Amanda, was that Big Gandhi could come back now because he was so perfect. And they knew too, Web said, that when he arrived he would make them all perfect just like himself. But only because they had breeding, Web cautioned. Just like Dremmel, Blake, Georgie and Web himself, Amanda would be safe because Big Gandhi would see to her safety after his return. She had breeding too, after all. So all she had to do now was just wait and be good while she waited, Web said. She shouldn't, for example, try to climb out over the wall inside her bedroom.

That left Amanda wondering why she would ever try to climb out over the wall inside her bedroom, and wondering, after Web's strange example, what other extreme activities they expected her to avoid in the service of safety and goodness.

Then later, Blake pulled her aside. He looked drained of his usual boisterous energy. Blake told Amanda that he knew the most about what was now happening, because only he had heard the full list of pronouncements made by Macklam and Green. They had spoken mysterious words, he said, and you had to have heard them all to know that some of what they had said was misleading and meant to deceive – perhaps to confuse them and disguise from them the high stature and power that their breeding bestowed, Blake conjectured. For example, he said to Amanda, Debbie Green had described Georgie in a way that really was closer to a description of Blake himself. And, Blake continued, Debbie Green's description of Blake himself would have sounded to anyone in the world like a closer description of Georgie. In fact, anyone who knows both Georgie and Blake would have seen right away that Debbie Green had deliberately switched her descriptions of them. If anyone doubted it, they could see right away that she wasn't being honest from other things she said, especially the things that she said about Web. She made Web out to be some kind of a superhero, which had to prove that she had been trying to throw off any listeners, said Blake. In addition to that, both Macklam and Green said opposite things about Dremmel, with Green saying Dremmel was great and Macklam saying Dremmel was not so great – though Blake could see that Macklam's picture was the accurate one. And you would expect just that, Blake noted, because Macklam is more powerful than Debbie Green.

Blake reiterated that only he had heard all the descriptions, so he alone saw very clearly how Macklam and Green had been trying to trick him to make him doubt that Big Gandhi is really coming back. But Blake told Amanda that we wasn't fooled. He said that he knew Big Gandhi was going to return, because just like Blake himself, Big Gandhi had breeding. And like

Blake himself, Big Gandhi could follow all the commands just perfectly – especially commands about running and jumping. Things like that were important, Blake said to Amanda. He would teach her to follow commands too, Blake emphasized. He would start right away. Well, maybe not right away, but at least before Big Gandhi came back. He would start her lessons soon, he assured her, especially since Macklam and Green had been so careful to conceal the exact date of Big Gandhi's return.

The talk left Amanda wondering, what was the full set of stunts and behaviors she now was expected to perform? Jumping must be okay, she reasoned, as long as she didn't jump over her bedroom wall. But there had to be more she should do than just run and jump.

At last Dremmel got her alone. He said that the others didn't understand the whole story. He had figured it out, he said, from what he personally had heard Debbie Green and Macklam announce. After thinking a lot about it, Dremmel said, he understood that Big Gandhi was coming back because he was born to be here.

"That might sound kind of simple at first," Dremmel explained. "But that's exactly what breeding means. It means privilege. Remember how we knew everything about Big Gandhi before we even met him? We knew as soon as we got here. We knew right away how special he is and how important he is. I was the one who first found out about him, by the way. I sniffed him out right here at this fence almost as soon as I got here. But that's the thing: this place was made for him. That's why it's so nice. It's a privilege to have this great big yard that's so clean and open like this. It's a privilege to have such a comfortable home. Those others over there don't have this, do they? You don't see those nonnies living in such a perfect place. We have it because of breeding. Big Gandhi had breeding and he was here and now we have breeding and we're here. And now Big Gandhi is coming back, so that just proves what I'm saying."

"But where did he go?" Amanda asked Dremmel.

"Well, that's something that I don't know exactly. That's something that we have to wait until he gets back to find out. But one thing I know for sure, one thing that's as clear as can be, is that he left so he can come back. We know that because he *is* coming back. It proves it. It's the new way and Big Gandhi is the first one. It used to be that everyone sooner or later just vanished. But now Big Gandhi is coming back. All we have to do now is sit tight and stay here until he gets back. Because we have breeding too. That's the thing you have to remember, Amanda. You have all this privilege because of your breeding, so you have to pay attention to it. You have to protect it. That means you have to be the way you're supposed to be. We're different from the nonnies. Especially those two over there. They'll still vanish. They'll still go away to who knows where. And *they* won't come back. But with our breeding now we're safe. We have more privilege than they do. A lot more. We get to stay here in this place, because it's the best place there ever could possibly be. It's our place. Just look at how great it is!"

"But then how come Rin gets to be Bill Gates' dog?" Amanda puzzled.

"Forget about Rin," said Dremmel emphatically. "He's not Bill Gates' dog. Not anymore. That's what we know now. That's what we just found out: he's not Bill Gates' dog anymore. Big Gandhi is coming back because Big Gandhi is better. We heard Macklam and Debbie Green say exactly that."

"So Big Gandhi will be the new Bill Gates' dog?"

"Well, yeah. I guess so. I didn't really think of it that way. I think it's more like, we'll all be Bill Gates' dogs, because we all have breeding. It's the breeding that makes Big Gandhi better, and that's what we have. That's why you can't have anything to do with that Rin and that other one over there. What's her name?"

"Ester."

"Right. Ester. Whatever you do, don't have anything more to do with that Rin or that Ester. You don't want to vanish like they will. You don't want to risk that. Don't even talk to them anymore. It could ruin everything for you."

Amanda did not understand how even just talking to Ester and Rin could jeopardize her safety. She enjoyed talking to them. She had grown to anticipate small conversations that lately had passed between Ester and her. The old woman was calming. She was courteous too. Plus old Ester's small and quiet wisdom, so unambitious, warmed Amanda with novel verities that tickled her with wonderment and awe, even though she did not fully grasp the merit of each truth – like Ester's gentle ravings on the springtime calls of mated birds at dawn. And though Amanda saw Rin only seldomly, his tossed-off greetings cheered her whenever they passed. She found herself too eagerly awaiting their next roundabout encounter out in their yards. She found herself obsessing about the prospect of another day at the lodge or lake or forest spent with Rin.

But Dremmel's warnings had been so emphatic. Dremmel had conveyed so much pat certainty that now she could not shake the fear of substantial reprisals if she violated his rules. Because they weren't Dremmel's rules, after all. At least they didn't' seem to be. Dremmel just understood them all so much better than she did. But the rules themselves came from higher. That's how they seemed. They seemed decreed from her unavoidable circumstance, from her breeding. The rules bore more authority than the simple pleasures of her conversations. At least they seemed to. She felt confused and saddened. Seeking solitude, she skulked into her house. She moped alone in shadows until Macklam found her there.

"Amanda, what are you doing inside all alone today?" he said to her. "It's far too nice a day for this. Come on. The boss is tied up today so Rin has some time off. I'm taking him out back for a run. It looks to me like you could use some fresh air too. Come on now. I think we'll bring old Ester with us, too. She's kind of like you today: she looks like she could use a stretch."

What! A walk with Rin! Amanda had been waiting so eagerly exactly for this chance. But wait. A walk with Rin? Her spontaneous excitement drained instantly away. She wasn't allowed even to speak with Rin. Nor speak with old Ester, either. How could she walk in the woods with them without even uttering a word? She would have to ignore them. What joy in that? What sense in even going along? What sense in keeping any kind of inner expectation of a friendship or companionship from outcasts who were unlike her? Yet Ester and Rin didn't seem so very different to her. Except for the circumstance that Dremmel called breeding, they didn't seem different at all. Yet breeding was privilege. Dremmel had been very certain of that and, looking around, she agreed that his assertion was impossible to deny. She lived very comfortably. What's more, now that Macklam had announced that Big Gandhi was returning, Dremmel assured her that she would continue to live quite comfortably. Ester and Rin would vanish. But oh, she would miss them. She felt instantly sorry that they would leave here, and leave her.

"Come on now," Macklam repeated.

She had no choice but to follow him. She went reluctantly, rising with labor and stepping lowly and stooped through her apartment door as Macklam held it open so she could pass to the big outer room that still was jumbled with Debbie Green's stuff. Macklam fetched Ester and Rin and led the three of them through the work room to the big exit door. Once outside of their building, Amanda felt exposed. She felt timid and insecure. Macklam brought them around the side of the building. They walked past it. As they skirted the chain link fencing that closed off their yards, Amanda yearned to return to the surety and security she knew inside the familiar bounds. But Macklam strode forward. He pushed up a knoll that rose beyond the back of their fenced neighborhood. From their yards the hill blocked off their view of the landscape that stood just over its bare, open crest. On other days, looking out from inside, Amanda had tried to imagine what she would find over the hill's hidden side. But today she shrunk back. Rin walked eagerly ahead of her with Macklam. Amanda felt frightened of him. At the same time she felt ashamed that he would see her reluctance. Old Ester walked in the back with Amanda, stiff legged and hobbled. She turned her head and shined a grin toward Amanda, who pretended not to notice as she minced her steps to stay well in back of Macklam and Rin.

At the top of the rise Macklam stopped and looked back at Amanda and Ester. "Come on, you two girls," he said to them. "It's downhill on this next side." He laughed. "The other day Rin and I went out in this direction for one of our walks. We hadn't tried this route before. We found an old rail bed a little ways into the woods down there. It's not too far off. There's not much there anymore but it's a clear and open trail. Let's follow it a little farther today, a little farther than Rin and I went before, just to see where it leads."

But she stayed well behind, walking slowly still, as Macklam turned and disappeared behind the hill top. When she crested the rise herself and saw him again, Amanda peered ahead of Macklam to try to spot Rin. But Rin had already disappeared into the vertical bank of forest below. Amanda felt anxious to bust through the green wall herself to discover Rin inside the dense woods. But what would she say to him? She stayed back behind Macklam, lagging slowly with Ester. Together they entered the trees below the hill at the spot where Macklam had disappeared ahead of them, at a trail opening that showed as a rut worn in the soil. Ester slowed and dropped several steps behind Amanda. After they walked a short distance among the trees they came upon Macklam, who had turned obliquely from the trail and stood there to wait for them.

"I'm just stopping to have a pee," he said. "You girls can keep going. You can see the path clearly enough. Just follow Rin."

But Rin had already doubled back. As the ladies walked forward they saw him on the path ahead of them, peering back quizzically. He called to them, "Is Macklam with you?"

At first Amanda did not answer, averting her eyes by focusing down at the path. But Rin asked the question again and she realized that Ester was panting too hard to comfortably reply. Amanda called back, "He's right behind us. He just had to stop for a minute."

"Okay," answered Rin. "I just wanted to make sure that this is the way he wants to take. Sometimes he changes his mind."

Amanda stayed silent. She felt both regret and relief when Rin turned up the trail again and resumed his fast stride out ahead of them.

"You don't have to walk back here with me," Ester said to her. "I'll be okay if you want to run up there with Rin."

Amanda felt embarrassed. "This is alright," she said quietly.

"This is all so surprising," Ester said. "I never expected to go so slowly. I get out so seldom now. In fact, it's been quite a while since I've been out for a long walk like this. I was so happy when Macklam asked me along. I never thought I'd get this tired."

Amanda stayed silent. After a moment Ester said, "Why don't you run up there with Rin? You'll have a better time."

"I don't mind this," Amanda replied softly.

Further along the trail Ester stopped.

"I just need to rest for a moment," she said. Amanda waited with her, watching while big breaths wheezed through Ester's body. When at last the air came more calmly, Ester said to Amanda, "It really is nice of you to stay here with me. I know you'd rather be up there with Rin. I'd rather be up there with him too. I never thought I would get so tired."

She rested a moment longer.

"I don't know if I should move on now or if I should just stay here and rest a while longer," Ester said. "It's very nice of you to stay here with me."

Amanda regarded her companion carefully before she said to Ester, "Let's stay here a little longer. I could use a little more rest myself."

"When we left I felt so happy for you," Ester said. "I thought you were going to have so much fun running up there with Rin."

"I don't mind this," Amanda responded.

"Are you feeling all right yourself?" Ester asked her.

Amanda looked down the trail in the direction they had come. "I guess Macklam will be catching up pretty soon," she said.

"Maybe," said Ester. "But Rin told me that sometimes he likes to stop and look at things when they walk. He might be a ways behind us yet. You don't seem to be yourself today, Amanda."

"I'm okay."

"Are you feeling ill?"

"No."

"Is something bothering you?"

"Not really."

"Thank you for waiting here with me," said Ester. "I have to be honest and tell you I feel a lot safer because you're here with me. I've never felt so tired. I've never had so much trouble just catching my breath."

Amanda peered backward along the trail, hoping for Macklam to appear. Her concern grew silently.

"It's still awfully nice to be out," Ester said in the quiet. "I've never been out here before. The woods are so beautiful."

"Do you like living back there at your house?" Amanda asked her spontaneously.

"I like it very much," Ester answered. "I feel very comfortable there. I like having Rin with me, too. Even though he's so young he's polite and he's patient. Just like you. He helps me a lot whenever he's around. I know you like him, too. I was so happy that you were coming along with us today. I thought you'd be running up there with Rin and having a much better time than this. I figured I would lag behind a little, but I never thought I would get as tired as this."

"It's okay," said Amanda. "It's kind of nice to just wait here and talk." Then, after a moment, she dared the question, "Why do people suddenly just disappear?"

"I don't know that it's so sudden," Ester said.

"Do you know Dremmel? He's one of the guys who lives on the other side of me. He talks about it all the time, how you live some place and you're happy but you never know how long you'll be happy because you see so many people there with you who suddenly just vanish. They don't know they're going, because they don't talk about it in advance or anything. Nobody talks about it. They're just gone one day. You see that happen to everybody so you know it's going to happen to you, too. So it haunts you. That's what Dremmel talks about."

"You mean that he talks about going away someday?"

"Yeah, but not just going away. It's more like disappearing, like vanishing all the sudden and not having any control over it."

"But only frightened people want things to stay the way they are," replied Ester. "I've lived in a few different places."

"Did you know you would leave them?"

"I never thought about leaving. I felt happy while I was at each place. I feel happy now."

"But wasn't there one place where you were the happiest at? One where you wanted to stay at more than all the other places?"

"Look at me," Ester said. "I'm old."

"But it happens to young people too," Amanda said with some alarm. "I've had it happen to me. My brothers and sisters all disappeared one by one. Then I did too. I came here."

"Are you happy here?" Ester asked here.

"I'd like to stay here," Amanda said.

"What about Dremmel? Do you think he's happy?"

Amanda thought. "No, Dremmel doesn't seem to be very happy at all," she replied.

"Then he won't be happy any place, whether he leaves or stays."

Rin had doubled back again to check on the two ladies. From ahead of them on the path, he called back to them, "Hey, you two, I didn't think I was ever going to find you. Why'd you stop way back here? This is supposed to be a hike, you know, not a picnic."

Amanda answered him to spare Ester the effort: "We just needed to rest."

But Ester added: "I think we're ready to get moving now."

"We thought maybe we should wait for Macklam," said Amanda, trying to con a few more moments of rest for Ester.

But Rin said, "You don't have to wait for Macklam. He's always way behind me. He always sees things along the way and he likes to stop and look them over for a while. He catches up sooner or later. I stay on the right trail because I know where he wants to go. Today we're headed out to explore that old train path some more. We found it the other day. I was all the way there, I was ready to start exploring it and stuff, but then I thought I should run back to see where you two were."

"You can keep going ahead," Ester said, speaking loudly to disguise her faintness. "We're ready to start moving now. We won't be far behind you."

"Okay. Just remember that you don't have to worry about Macklam. He looks after himself just fine. I'll meet you up ahead where this trail joins into the rail line. I have to look around there for a few minutes anyway, to figure out which way we want to go."

Amanda and Ester resumed their measured pace as Rin scampered ahead again and disappeared with several bounds among trees that enfolded the path.

Ester smiled as she said, "He gets a little bit too caught up in his work sometimes, but that's because he's so young."

As they plodded together through the silent woods, Amanda felt Ester dragging her backward like a tethered weight as Ester's legs moved progressively slower. The tarried pace grew too awkwardly slow, too unnatural and uncomfortable for Amanda. She stopped to wait for Ester to close the gap that had opened between them on the trail.

Ester, breathing in labored drafts, had to draw very close to Amanda to tell her, "Just go ahead." She paused while her lungs clawed for air. "There's no sense in you staying way back here with me. I want you to run ahead with Rin. I'm okay. I really am. I can keep moving at this pace, but it's way too slow for you."

"Just rest for a minute," said Amanda. "Don't try to talk so much."

"But I need you to listen," wheezed Ester. "I want you to go ahead with Rin."

"I don't mind staying back," Amanda replied.

"But this is too slow for you. It's okay for me. I can keep going like this till I get there, but not if I think that I'm holding you up. I'm trying to go too fast because I don't want you to wait for me. That's making it worse. It will be better for me if you just run ahead with Rin. It'll be better for you too. It'll be better for both of us."

Desire pushed Amanda forward in spite of her concern for old Ester. But she also felt stammering uncertainty about how she might approach Rin. She wondered how she would behave with him, and what she might say if she suddenly drew up beside him on the trail ahead.

"If you don't catch up with him, he's just going to run back here again anyway," Ester went on with effort. "I don't want to be holding up the both of you. I'm moving okay now. I don't need you right next to me anymore. I'll feel a lot better if I'm not holding you up. I'll feel better if I know Rin's not going to come running back."

"Are you sure you're okay?" asked Amanda.

"Yes, I'm very sure I'm okay," Ester answered. "Macklam's not far behind me anyway. I want you to catch Rin and tell him not to worry about me. Tell him I'm coming along. It's just taking me longer than I expected it to."

Amanda caught up with Rin at the abandoned rail line. After she relayed Ester's assurance, the pair pushed forward eagerly. Rin decided they should follow the cut north to see what lay in that direction. They were far enough ahead of the others to return and explore the southern direction if, after a distance, they didn't find anything interesting.

The old rail bed was a widened lane that did not follow the land's contours like the foot trail that Amanda had just left. Instead it was leveled with fills and cuts meant to even the gradient so that, once upon a time, trains could travel it easily. The rails had long been removed and the wooden ties appeared occasionally in rotting heaps where they had been piled alongside the right-of-way. The ties were largely disintegrated. Unlike the winding foot trail, the rail cut ran straight. It was overgrown with grasses and weeds that were scored by narrowly spaced, parallel ruts made by dirt bikes and four-wheeled joy-riding scooters. Amanda and Rin scampered along the pathway with pent anticipation. Buoyed by their eagerness and engaged by their adventure, they followed the trail for what seemed like a short distance before the land appeared to flatten beside them and the trail widened through a broad swath of level landscape. The trees had once been cleared here. The saplings and scrub that filled in the clearing grew dense and abundant. The ruts that Amanda and Rin had been following, the ruts made by motorized runners, ran straight on ahead through the clearing. But on one side of the trail Rin noticed a leaning signal post just barely apparent among the ascending green bracken.

"I wonder why nobody's followed this," he said. "It looks like an old signal or sign. Look, we can veer off this way."

They cut away from the the wheel ruts and pushed through tall grasses and densely tangled brush until they emerged and saw running in front of them a second abandoned rail bed that once had been a siding that paralleled the primary train tracks. The siding seemed more thoroughly abandoned. It lacked any ruts made by ripping joy-riders. Grasses grew stubbly and short still because the ground beneath the siding had once been so densely packed. Amanda and Rin walked along their discovery until the clearing that surrounded them widened still more. The landscape there was dotted, mottled with stands of taller trees and drifts of lower shrubbery and then some open gaps where nothing appeared to grow at all. Rin and Amanda turned away from the siding and plunged into the overgrown clearing.

"There used to be a road running this way," said Rin as he dashed away from the rail-track bed. "Look, you can see how it used to run in a line. You can still see some asphalt underneath us here. It's all crumbled up but you can see it under all these big weeds."

Deeper into the clearing they made out the lines of other roads. Along the roads they saw that the blank spots, the places where no vegetation cut into the sky, were old cellar holes. Once upon a time homes and probably other structures had stood above them. But now the pits sank as sumps filled with reeds that pushed up among scummy green pods on captured water.

"This used to be a little town once," said Rin. "But look at it now.

There's nothing left. You wouldn't know there was anything here unless you stood in the middle of it right like this. I bet that in a few more years you won't be able to tell at all. It'll all be just woods by then."

"I wonder where everybody went," said Amanda.

"Who knows. They sure didn't leave much behind."

"They left the roads and they left all their houses," Amanda said. "Look: you can still see some of the wood down in these cellars. It looks like all the houses just rotted away and collapsed. There's still some big beams down there. They haven't all rotted away yet."

"But they're rotting away fast," said Rin. "Give it a little while longer and, like I said, you'll never know anything was here. The forest will take it all."

"I wonder when they went away," Amanda mused. "Do you think they left a long time ago?"

"I don't know. Not too long. These trees aren't very big. They're not nearly as big as the rest of the trees out there in the woods. So I bet it wasn't all that long ago. And I bet it won't be too much longer before there's no trace at all. Then it will just be the woods. Then all these things here now that people once built will be gone."

"I kind of like it like this," said Amanda. "It's kind of more interesting now when there's just a little bit left. You see how things change."

"I know. I like it the most when it's like this, too, when things are still just growing up and filling in and everything," said Rin. "When it's just a big jumble and tangle of things. It's like it's more alive. That's what Ester told me once when I was telling her about things I find when I'm out walking with Macklam. She said she used to find a lot of places like this, too. They're everywhere – places where all the plants are still just growing back, where they're still filling in after a farm or a building or something like this whole town used to be here. She told me places are more teeming and alive when they're like this, when everything is growing fast and fighting for space, than they are when they're all filled in and old."

"I wonder how Ester is doing now," Amanda put in.

"That's a good question," said Rin. "She and Macklam should have caught up by now, because we've been looking around here for quite a while already. I think maybe we better run back and get them. We can bring them back here and show them. We can look around some more ourselves. Macklam is going to love this place. I think Ester will like it too."

They hustled back along the rail bed to the spot where their first trail had emerged from the woods. They turned in hastily, surprised and a little alarmed that they hadn't yet met Macklam and Ester coming forward. They went back almost to the place where Amanda and Ester had parted. They found Ester laying in a small hollow several steps off the side of the wooded trail. Macklam was crouched beside her, patting her gently. Ester drew breaths in long, gulping wheezes that sounded weak despite the loud rasp that each breath made. Macklam looked up gravely at the pair as they approached.

"The poor girl must have been looking for a sheltered spot," he said quietly. "She turned off the trail on her own but this was as far as she could get. Still, I might have walked right past her if her breathing wasn't so loud. If this was me they'd call this congestive heart failure, and we might as well call it that for Ester too. Her lungs are filling up with fluid, poor thing."

Macklam stood up and surveyed the landscape around them. He looked forward along the trail, toward the abandoned rail bed. He turned and looked backward along the trail, toward their starting point near the kennel compound.

"I can't carry her all the way back," he said. "Especially not now when she feels this weak. But there's a dirt road that runs just beyond that little rise through the trees there. It's not too long a bushwhack to get to it. I can drive the Suburban in there and then we can carry her to the car and drive her out, poor girl. I'd better run back as fast as I can to the house to get the car right away. I'll get Debbie and a stretcher and we can carry poor Ester to the dirt road and then drive her back from there. You two had better come along with me too."

But when Macklam approached him, Rin planted his feet and snarled with an expression so forbidding that Macklam reeled backward a pace.

"Okay, okay" he said, "I should have known you wouldn't want to leave her alone out here. It's probably best that you stay with her anyway, although I guess it's bad form for me to let you make the decision like this. Under the circumstances I'm not going to fight you about it. You go ahead and stay here and look after her while I get the car."

Macklam turned to Amanda. "I suppose you want to stay too," he said. "All right. I'll get back here as quickly as I can."

By the time he returned with Debbie Green, Ester's breathing had grown erratic and even more labored. She could not speak, but her tortured eyes gazed pitiably at her companions. Her expression showed fear and startled confusion. They lifted her carefully onto the stretcher. They carried her slowly over the untrammeled ground to avoid jarring her. Inside the big Suburban, Macklam took time to settle her comfortably on her side across the long bench seat while the others loaded in. Rin sat at her head with gentle regard and heightened attention. Debbie Green wept quietly.

After the solemn ride home Macklam said to Debbie, "you get Rin and Amanda settled inside. I'll get Ester to the doctor right away and we'll see what he can do for her."

But Ester did not come back.

CHAPTER 12

At the untidy offices of the Habitat Defenders Fund, Marci Waters watched impatiently for Justin Bainbridge to arrive. He came in at last, strolling through the door casually at mid-morning as if he had entered a coffee shop. Marci greeted him at once and led him to the bare and windowless meeting room. Bainbridge slouched into a chair. He sat low, crossed his ankles and pushed his legs into a long stretch under the table.

"Justin, I really need to talk to you," Marci Waters began. "Last night I was going over the books again – you know, writing some checks and paying some bills and all that stuff – and after a while I really got worried. I mean, I get worried about it all the time, but this time it seems worse than usual. I've been talking to some of our donors – you know, the big money guys like the Sierra Club and the Wildlife fund and all of those big groups. I've got grants pending with all of them. I mean grant applications – I don't know if I'll ever actually get the grants. That's the thing: they've been telling me how tough it's getting out there. How competitive, I mean. There's so many groups like us. They send in so many requests for money. That's what they're telling me. They have to spread it out more. So it's not so certain I can get as much money from them anymore."

"What, you mean the Sierra Club doesn't want to support any of our programs anymore?" Bainbridge asked.

"They want to," Waters answered. "It's just that there's a lot of groups, a lot of different priorities today. So they examine everything so much more carefully. So that even when I do get a grant, it's such a long wait before I get the actual money. From the government especially. I mean, they take so long to process all the applications. But I've got bills that I've gotta pay now. Right now. Do you know what I mean?"

"I know exactly what you mean," chimed Bainbridge.

"That's why I think we could use more visibility," Marci Waters continued. "I thought of that last night when I got so worried about all the bills. About money. If we make ourselves more visible, you know, make people more aware of us, it could really move us up the list. You know, make us a higher priority so we get more funding. More money."

"I'm all for that," Bainbridge said.

"So I was wondering how your Gates Foundation thing is going."

"Well the Gates Foundation already turned down our grant request. I already told you all about that."

"I know," said Waters. "But you said you were going to look for a way to, you know, to turn up the heat on them a little. You said you were going to make them sweat. That was how you put it."

"Oh, that," said Bainbridge. "I'm still working on that."

"But that's what I'm wondering," Waters pressed on. "I'm wondering if you've gotten anywhere on it yet. Because the visibility it gives us could be really important. I mean, even if you don't get anything from the Gates Foundation, just going after them a little, you know, just stirring up some controversy and stuff and just getting our name out there might really help with our visibility. I don't want you to do anything bad. I mean, like when we talked about it before, I said you had to be careful because, to a lot of people, the Gates Foundation *is* charity. It's got a really good reputation and everything. But that's just the point: they've made themselves really, really visible. So if we go after them, it's going to improve our visibility, too."

"Yeah, they're as visible as hell," said Bainbridge. "That's the one thing I found out: they've really done a good job of building up their image. They've really done a lot of public relations and chased down all the right people and everything. They got everyone on their side. Everyone thinks they're great."

"That's why you have to be careful," she repeated. "But if there really was something to say . . ., I mean, if you really did find some really good, really legitimate reason to protest and, you know, stir up some controversy, it would help us a lot. It would put us more on the map, so that raising money would get easier for us. So that when I ask for donations and grants and everything, people will already know who we are."

"Well I don't have anything just yet," he explained. "I only had one meeting, so I'm just getting started. But right now I'm thinking of going to Amsterdam with my girlfriend, so I might have to put it off for a while."

"Amsterdam? Put it off? But Justin, you said you were really pissed off about this."

"I was. I still am. I'm really pissed off."

"Who was your meeting with?"

"With this guy at the Times. I can't remember his name. But Paul Eldad, right? His girlfriend works at the New York Times, right? She's only a copy editor, but she set us up with this guy who used to write a lot about Microsoft. He's a business reporter. He goes way back. He's probably about sixty years old or something."

"But, Justin," she interrupted, "we talked about this before: it isn't about Microsoft. It's about the Bill and Melinda Gates Foundation. They're the ones who give the grants. Microsoft is the company that Bill Gates started. Sure, that's how he made all his money. But then he used a ton of it to start the Gates Foundation. That's what we care about: the foundation."

"I know that's what we care about. Ya gotta let me finish, Marci. I'm not talkin' about Microsoft. I'm talkin' about Bill Gates. He controls the foundation, right? He runs the whole damn thing. That's what I was talking to this reporter about: not about Microsoft, but about Bill Gates."

"Okay, Justin. Sorry."

"We were talking about Bill Gates. Turns out this reporter is pretty pissed off at him too. Not pissed off like me. It's more like, he can't believe Bill Gates suddenly turned around and made himself into some kind of hero. It used to be a lot different. That's what this reporter told me. That's why this meeting was so interesting. He said that if you go back not too long ago, everybody thought of Bill Gates as kind of a crooked businessman. Maybe not crooked, exactly. But kind of like, you know, this money-grubbing guy. This cut-throat wheedler. Kind of a swindler and a double-crosser. Nobody trusted him. In fact, going back a little ways, there were all sorts of law suits and legal settlements and everything. That's what this guy told me, this reporter. He named all sorts of companies that Microsoft robbed – that Bill Gates robbed. They were companies I never heard of before, Wang and Digital Equipment and some others. I can't remember, but this guy sure knew about them. He said that it wasn't too long ago that if you did something in the computer business and if Bill Gates set his eyes on what you were doing, if Bill Gates wanted Microsoft to do whatever it was you were doing with computers, you were screwed. Absolutely screwed. 'Cause Bill Gates would rob you. That's what this reporter said."

Bainbridge pushed upright out of his slouch , sucking his legs tightly under his chair and leaning forward to prop his forearms on the table top. He ticked his right leg rapidly so that his knee bounced.

"But then Gates turned everything around," he continued. "That's what's got this guy so pissed off. Maybe not pissed off. Maybe, I don't know, maybe *frustrated* is the right word for it. He told me that it seemed like all the sudden Bill Gates realized that the only thing that history is going to remember his as is this cut-throat, shady businessman. So instead of putting all his efforts into making more money, he started putting all his efforts into changing his image. Hell, he already had more money than anyone could ever spend anyway. He was already the richest guy in the world. He didn't need any more. So he took a huge pile of money and he started the Bill and Melinda Gates Foundation – starring Bill and Melinda Gates, of course. Don't get me wrong, he's still got a huge pile of money for himself. I mean, it's not like he's giving everything away and suddenly he's a hobo or a monk or something. He's still the richest guy around. But now he spends those riches trying to make himself look good."

"Okay, Justin, I get all that," said Marci. "But other than some shady deals way back in the past, what's all of that mean for us?"

"I don't know. Well, I kind of know, but I just don't know what to do about it yet. I mean, I haven't really worked up any kind of plan or anything."

"Besides," griped Waters, "it sounds like all the so-called dirt you dug up isn't even about the Gates Foundation. It's about Bill Gates, sure. But it's all Microsoft stuff and it's all ancient history."

"Yeah, but you can't go after a foundation. You gotta go after a guy. You have to make it personal, put a name and a face on it so people can relate to it. Everybody knows that. It's like, if they taught a Protest 101 class in college, that's what they would tell you. That's why I'm talkin' to this guy at the Times about Bill Gates. We gotta get to *him*. To Bill Gates himself."

"Okay. But it still doesn't sound like you got anything."

"But I only just started, Marci. I mean, what the fuck. Ya gotta give a guy a chance. And besides, there's this one more thing, this one little angle

I'm still working."

"Well, okay, what is it?" asked Waters.

"It's his damn dog," said Bainbridge. "You remember that newspaper article I showed you from the Times? That big, long article about Gates? Well, I showed the same article to the reporter. He hadn't read it before but he read it when I showed it to him. He said it was kind of funny because it talked all about this thing that Gates' calls thinking week. But the only thing Gates does during his thinking week is read reports about other people's ideas. People from Microsoft. That's not really thinking, this guy said. At least it's not original thinking. So why call it thinking week?"

"But what about the dog, Justin?"

"Remember the article had this bit in it about Gates being an animal lover and having this dog lying at his feet and everything? The reporter said that in all his investigations and his interviews of Gates and everything, there was never any kind of hints of anything about dogs."

"So?"

"So it just got me thinking that, if this guy's such a dog lover and everything, why isn't he doing anything for animal rights? I mean, we're the ultimate in animal rights, right? The Habitat Defenders Fund is all animal. We're trying to get the humans the hell out of their way. Give them back the places we took. We have a valid claim on all that money he's throwing around."

"Sure we do," said Waters. "But I don't know if the connection is strong enough. We talked about that before, Justin. I don't know if you can say that, because Bill Gates has a dog, he should be giving us money."

"Well, like I said, I'm still working on it. But I can see putting together a protest that says, hey, this guy doesn't really care about animals. He doesn't even care about dogs. Probably he didn't even have a dog until he got one for this newspaper article and everything. The point is to embarrass him, right? To shame him, so he'll come around to our way of thinking and agree with us."

"But we don't even know for sure that he didn't have a dog before."

"But we can find that out," said Bainbridge. "I mean, we can hire somebody to run that down, to do all the legwork of looking in the records and talking to people and everything to find out if Bill Gates really did have dogs before. If he didn't, he's a fraud and that's what we'll shame him with."

"But who are you going to hire? I told you before, Justin, this is such a long shot that we're not going to pay a lot of money for it."

"And I told you before that I'll cover it. Me and Carl and a couple of others. We'll hire the investigative. . ., the investigative . . ., the investigator to look into it. We just got to get the forms from you, the tax forms so we can deduct it as a charitable contribution to a non-profit. But that's no problem, right?"

"And what if your suspicion turns out to be true and Bill Gates isn't really a dog lover? What are you going to do then?"

"Then I'll plan a protest. You know: some signs, and some printed brochures that say why he's a fraud. That say that it's all about publicity and not really about the animals or anything."

"But you have to be careful, Justin. I mean, you have to be careful about what you do and where you do it. Especially where. I mean, at the wrong place you might not get any attention at all. Or even worse, you might only get negative publicity. I'd say go for a campus. Protests always get traction on campuses. Even better, go for an Ivy League school. We always do the best at those. If he's gonna be at any Ivy League schools any time soon, that would be perfect."

"Okay," said Bainbridge. "I can try to find out his schedule, too."

"I know it's a long shot, but, hey, you never know."

"That's what I say."

"And be careful about how you do it, too," she warned. "I mean, it should be an informational protest. I mean, signs and brochures are great, but not a lot of screaming."

"But I like screaming," Bainbridge quipped.

"But this isn't the right forum," she corrected.

"I know, I know. I was just kidding."

"That means you have to be careful about who you hire to carry the signs and pass out the papers and everything. I mean, no one too extreme."

"Don't worry," he said.

"But when can you do all this, Justin?"

"When? I don't know. I'm working on it now."

"I know. But you also said you're going to Amsterdam. Which is it, Justin? I mean, first you were saying how important this was, then you were saying you'll put it off so you can go to Amsterdam with your girlfriend."

"Okay," he conceded, "I'll get going on it right away. I'll talk to my girlfriend about maybe putting off the trip for a little bit. But she's going to be pissed. I mean, Amsterdam's about the coolest place on earth."

"Thanks, Justin," said Waters. "We really need the visibility right now. It will really help our fund-raising. So stay in touch and let me know how you're making out with this."

CHAPTER 13

Cassie Welch popped into the small and spotless office in which Albert Wistol worked. Wistol, the publicity reader who searched the media to gauge the public image that Bill Gates was building, stayed hard at his computer screen, not noticing the woman as she leaned casually against his door post. When she lifted her coffee cup and sipped, he looked up at last.

"I hear you're hitching a ride on the corporate jet," Welch said to him.

"Oh, hi. Yeah. I'm flying out with them tomorrow. Hey, I didn't know you were going to be here today."

"Yeah, I just came out of a meeting with Melinda. Just the usual stuff," said Cassie Welch, the image consultant to Melinda Gates. "There wasn't too much to talk about. I have a suspicion this project is going to start winding down soon. It should, anyway, because it looks like we're close to meeting our goals. I don't think the Gates will want to keep us on after that. They're very goal-oriented, project oriented. I haven't talked to Franklin yet to see if he feels the same way. But after reading your last few reports, after seeing how Bill's image has turned around, I don't see how anyone could reach a different conclusion. It looks like he's doing really well."

"So you think they'll just close down the whole project?" asked Wistol, suddenly concerned about losing his job. He knew that, with agency work, employment followed your team. If your team wrapped up a job, you could wait on furlough until another contract came up.

"I doubt if they'll close the whole project down," Welch replied. "At least not at first. But I think there's a good chance they'll scale it back. We're getting near the end of the real intense part. That's pretty typical in this business: you have an intense phase in a project when you're at it twenty-four hours a day. But that doesn't last forever. As you start to accomplish your objectives – as you start to create the image you're aiming for – the work starts to diminish. There's just not as much to do anymore. It doesn't stop right away. But the project scales back. That's when I start looking for my next client."

"Do you really think we're there yet?" Wistol asked as he grew more anxious.

"I think we're getting very close. Your own reports show that. Bill's public image continues to turn very favorable. Melinda's too, although it was always Bill's that mattered the most. Not to belittle Melinda, of course. Technically, she's my client, while Franklin is handling Bill. But we've always focused mostly on Bill, because his background and his history with Microsoft and everything gives him a lot more public presence. We always knew that Melinda's image would more or less follow along after Bill's. And it was Bill's image that needed the big turn-around in the first place. I have to say that it's gone really well. It's gone better than I ever expected. I mean, I expected us to succeed, but it seems like every little effort we've made has paid off. Even the dog idea. That was Franklin's and at first I thought it was crazy. I mean, it made some sense on paper. And it's true that the small, subtle things you do can really accumulate and end up doing a lot to improve a client's public persona. But I just didn't think we'd ever be able to pull off an image dog. But now you've found it in a few places, where some reporting about this dog next to Bill kind-of softens his image and makes him look more human. It's subtle, but it counts."

"Oh, God, I just wish it wasn't a dog," complained Wistol.

"Yeah, it's too bad they make you so nervous," Welch replied. "I thought you were off the hook after that first one bombed out. Remember that? What was his name? Gandhi, I think. Bill didn't want to have anything to do with that dog and I figured the whole thing was over after that. Too bad for you we tried it again. Who would have thought this second dog would have worked out so well. It's almost like Bill even likes having him around now. What's the new one's name? Rin, I think."

"Yeah, it's Rin all right," Wistol said. "God, he seems to be everywhere now."

"That's what I was just wondering about. I just heard that you're going along on the corporate jet to Boston tomorrow."

"That's where I'm from," explained Wistol. "Bill is flying there to give the Harvard speech and I'm going along just to visit my parents while he's there. They're really generous to let me go along on the corporate jet like that."

"But did you know that he's taking Rin?" Welch asked. "Rin will be on the plane with you."

"Oh, God, I didn't know," moaned Wistol.

"That's what I mean: it's almost like Bill likes having him around now. But to tell you the truth, that whole program has gone so well that being with Rin around Harvard and Boston makes a lot of sense from an image viewpoint, too."

* * *

But at Harvard a surprise awaited Gates and the image builders. The business reporter from the New York Times, the same Microsoft dissenter who earlier had briefed Justin Bainbridge of the Habitat Defenders Fund about all his historic suspicions regarding the software giant, had stumbled into information about the image dog. Separately, the reporter had been working on an article about image consulting in general, about the whole hidden business of buffing the public esteem of clients by building them up in the media. While interviewing insiders for the article, he had encountered one reputation maker who told the reporter about the image dog. She told him how members of her name-making profession now bruited about Bill Gates' dog. She explained how image consultants everywhere suddenly spoke of the canine as a winning example of subtle association, showing how even a pet can promote a positive image for a client. In her trade it was thought of as brilliant, she told the reporter. The reporter quite naturally, though confidentially, relayed his discovery to Justin Bainbridge of the Habitat Defenders Fund. Therefore, when Bill Gates arrived at the Harvard graduation celebration to deliver his commencement address and receive an honorary degree, protesters passed out leaflets that called him a fraud, revealing that he had acquired a dog only to improve his public standing. The next Sunday, the business reporter's long article about the aims and practices of the image-consulting industry appeared in the New York Times. It used Bill Gates' dog as a stunning example of the ways in which the business tries to turn public opinion.

CHAPTER 14

"**I** feel like I just got mugged," said Bill Gates as he sat at the big round table in the round conference room with his wife, Melinda, and with his image consultant Franklin Osborne, with Melinda's image expert Cassie Welch, and with the publicity reader Albert Wistol. Macklam also attended the meeting, but he stayed in the background in a chair along the wall. Removed a step, but dutifully near Gates' side sat Rin. Next to him was Amanda. Both Amanda and Rin had been heading out for a ramble with Macklam when the businesspeople had urgently gathered. Telephoned in haste, Macklam had led them both to the meeting, rather than lose time by taking Amanda back home.

But Macklam had been unaware of the Harvard pamphlets and the newspaper article and the subsequent blow-up over the image dog program. Therefore he had not realized that Rin and maybe Amanda too were to be the subjects of this sudden conference.

Albert Wistol had figured on Rin's attendance. In advance he had swallowed a prescribed dose of Xanax to help still his anxiety. He had run through breathing exercises, and he had carefully coached his own psyche to remain unfluttered in the presence of powerful Rin. He had entered the round conference room feeling buoyed by confidence that irrational fear would not shake him this time. He had even felt some swagger and some eagerness to show all the others at the meeting that he had beat the consumptive panic.

But Wistol had never imagined that Amanda would come along also and settle beside Rin. Secretly now he looked at her sidelong as she sat with composure and quiet diffidence next to Rin, the two of them close off the side of Bill Gates. Wistol encouraged himself by noting that at least Amanda wasn't quite as large as Rin. She was a hand smaller, slender and more dainty in her proportions than the male. That made her less intimidating, Wistol assured himself. But he couldn't chase the suspicion that, despite her tidier size, Amanda might still double his difficulty to keep composed. He struggled to subdue the rush of uncertainty as he wondered now if his preparations would hold.

"It's worse than a mugging," Gates went on. "It's like I set myself up for this whole disaster by agreeing to do this in the first place. The only reason we did it was to make me look genuine. Now it's doing exactly the opposite. How in the hell did that ever happen?"

"Maybe it wasn't such a good idea to begin with," said Melinda Gates.

"You thought it was a good idea at the time. At the time everyone thought it was a great idea and everyone said that the only thing I had to do was put in some time and effort and get used to having him around. But I did that. In fact I called Reginald here today to bring Rin here to prove that I did it. Look at him," said Gates as he gestured toward Rin. "It looks like we're the perfect pair, like we've been together for something like forever. But now instead of a genuine guy, I'm being called a fake. How in the hell did that happen, Frank?"

"We're as surprised as you are by it, Bill," answered Osborne. "Naturally we started a work-up as soon as it happened. We'll trace it all the way back to see what went wrong. We were doing great, just great, until now."

"I don't care how great you think we were doing," said Gates. "This blows it all up right now."

"Right," answered Osborne. "But we have to stay calm. We have to keep in mind that the most important thing we need to do now is to formulate a response. We need to execute that right away. In the meantime we'll work-up what went wrong and how this all got exposed. We need to avoid something like this at all costs in the future."

"The future!" Gates exclaimed. "We need to do something about this right now."

"Well, yes. Right now for the response," Osborne repeated. "We're doing that right now and that's what we're here to discuss. We have some ideas already and we're going to discuss them and execute them right away."

"You have to understand that this is very unusual," Cassie Welch put in. "We were doing so well, and everything was working out so perfectly. We had everyone on our side. The press. The philanthropic community. Every-one. At this stage in the game I never expected anything like this to happen. I mean, sure, anything can happen at any point, and we're certainly pre-pared for that anything. But at this stage of the game I never expected anything like this. And this thing with Rin was just a little side project anyway. I mean, we've done so much more, so many other big promotions and big projects and all. This image dog project was just an accent, a little side idea. I never thought this would be the one that would bite back and trip us up."

"I'd say it bit back pretty damn hard," Gates groused. "I'm ready to scrap the whole damn thing. I never should have started it. I should have stuck with my instincts."

"But we're already so far into it," said Welch. "Quitting now might not be the best idea. Think about it: what kind of message would that send? It would only be an admission of guilt. I think there's better ways to respond to this than just throwing up our hands and backing out. It's too late for that anyway."

Gates turned his head to look at Rin at his side.

"I'm not throwing up my hands," he said. "It's a solid business decision. We tried it. It failed. It's as simple as that. There's no sense in putting more work into it now. There's no sense in keeping him around."

Amanda suddenly shuddered. Her ears pricked at Gates' statement: "There's no sense in keeping him around." She canted her head and looked at Rin and prepared to ask him, "What does he mean?" But Rin silenced her with a glance. He had sat through so many meetings. He knew it was unfit for him or Amanda to speak.

"But you've already put in the work," Cassie Welch said to Gates. "I mean, the hard part is already done. Look at him and look at you right now. It's like you just said: you look as natural as can be together. He's just here with you and there's no more effort involved. What the heck, even Albert's gotten used to him by now." She gestured toward Wistol and chuckled inclusively. "It won't take any more work for you to just keep doing what you're doing, instead of just sending him off and forgetting all about him and admitting that what they're saying is right."

"But what they're saying *is* right," Melinda Gates corrected.

"Well, maybe," said Welch. "I mean, it's right right now. But you have to remember that there's a certain velocity to these things. Right now it's fresh and new and it seems like it's the biggest issue on earth and it has us here in this emergency meeting and everything. And we *should* be here to respond to it. I'm not saying there's anything wrong with that. But come back here in a week. Come back in a month. Two months. Three months. Come back this time next year and see if you even remember this whole thing happened. That's what I mean about velocity. It's a big deal right now because it just broke and now all the media is jumping on it. But those guys have an incredibly short memory. We talked about that before, remember: the institutional memory of the media is incredibly short. They'll hype something like it's the biggest issue on earth, but then they'll move on and you'll never see it mentioned again. That's one reason why quitting now may not be such a good idea. This will pass pretty fast. If you hold on and let it blow over, then you might still get some benefit from having Rin around. That positive image will build more over time and you'll get a better return out of all the work you've put in – once this blows over, I mean. Besides, if you get rid of Rin right now, you're going to give them another story. They'll report that now Bill Gates got rid of the dog, and that will just add another chapter and make the whole thing last longer than it will if you just leave it alone and pretend that nothing has happened."

"In the meantime we can counter any negative impact that might be coming from this," said Franklin Osborne, rushing in to keep from being too far over-spoken by his colleague Cassie Welch. "We can respond in the short term with some initiatives that can counteract any damage that may have been caused."

"What I need to know is just how bad *is* the damage," Gates demanded.

"Well of course, Albert's been following that," Osborne said. "Right, Al?"

"Right," said Albert Wistol. "I have it right here." As he plied his little laptop he felt bent two ways. He felt eager to speak, to draw eyes and come out from under cover in order to show the others that his defenses would hold. Yet he also felt afraid to speak and draw eyes. He felt uncertain and he questioned whether his new defenses would hold. "We all know about the first instances," he pushed on. "There was the leaflets at Harvard. That was really small. I mean, I'm sure I would have found something about it on the web, because so many people do so many little blogs and so naturally I found a few who wrote something about it. But they were really small and they would have been really, really low in any kind of search results if I didn't know exactly what to look for. I mean, the only reason I knew about it was because somebody at Harvard put one of the leaflets into Bill's hand when he was there. Otherwise it would have been hard to find out about it because the protest was so small and so localized and everything. Those kinds of things don't really have an impact because people are so used to all these special-interest groups making this claim or that claim. But the thing that really hurt us was the story in the New York Times. That had more weight because, well, it was the Times. But it wasn't really all that bad because the mention of Rin was just a small part inside a much bigger story about our whole brand-identity business. Our image-consulting business. I mean, it wasn't good, but it's not like the whole article was all about our image-dog program. It was just a couple of paragraphs inside a bigger article about something else."

"But how did it ever get in there?" interrupted Gates. "We're supposed to be building a positive image. That's the whole reason all of you are here. But then this comes out and it takes what you're doing and turns it into a negative image. Sure, the article in the Times didn't come out and say it, but in this pamphlet here it says in black and white that I'm a fraud. That's not much of a positive image, is it? How did they ever find out about this?"

Osborne and Wistol and Cassie Welch glanced roundly at each other.

"Well of course we looked into that right away," Osborne spoke. "We haven't been able to retrace the entire chain of events, at least not yet. But the general outline of what happened is pretty clear. It looks to us like this reporter was doing a routine story about this whole business of brand identity and image consulting and the lot. It was just a typical, in-depth, kind of focus-on article that you see all the time. And while he was interviewing people, you know, talking to people in our business about what we do, this must have come out. We don't know exactly who told him. He's pretty careful not to give that away in the article. He says something like … Albert can find the exact passage for us, but he says something like the image dog is being talked about as a successful program inside the business."

"That's exactly the problem," Gates cut in. "This shouldn't be talked about at all. It's supposed to be confidential. Everything we do is supposed to be strictly confidential. That was one of the first points we covered in our contract with you, because obviously none of this can work if everyone knows that there's people behind the scenes pulling strings. Then it ends up looking negative instead of positive, just like this thing now. The fact that people in your business are talking about this program is a breech of our contract."

Wistol, Osborne and Welch glanced at each other again.

"We don't think it's really being talked about by everybody," Cassie Welch began. "I mean, not like the way he makes it sound in the article. That's just a way these journalists have of presenting stuff and making it sound different than it really is."

"Well obviously somebody talked to him about it," Gates countered.

"We're trying to find out who might have known," explained Osborne. "We're trying to find out who might have told him because we're extremely careful about confidentiality. Because, well, like you said, Bill, our whole business depends on it. But there's a certain amount of paperwork. You know: reports and memos and things like that back at the agency, because we have to account for what we're doing here, of course. A certain number of people see those. And there's our creative team, of course. It meets at the agency and discusses specific projects and comes up with ideas. So there's people who know about everything we do. We're looking at recent departures from the agency and we're investigating who spoke to this reporter so we can find out who might have told him."

"What about this pamphlet?" Gates drove on. "How in the hell did this group that put out this pamphlet find out?"

"We're looking into that, too," said Osborne.

"Who in the hell are these people, anyway?" asked Gates. "I never even heard of the Habitat Defenders Fund."

"That much we know already," answered Cassie Welch. "The Habitat Defenders Fund is an animal rights group. We jumped right in and found out everything about them. They're a non-profit. Kind of a splinter group, I'd say. They're small, but like so many of these small groups, they're fiercely devoted to their cause. Those little groups are all kind of the same that way: one cause, but that cause is the whole universe to them, so they work at it non-stop and they hit really hard. They make a lot of noise. That makes them seem really big. It makes them seem more representative than they really are. We work with groups like that from time to time because when you get them on your side they can have a really big impact. We'd never work with these guys though. I mean, they're pretty extreme. They're extreme environmentalists who think that the whole problem is people. Like, if people would just go away then all the problems in the world would be solved. They're trying to restore things to the way they were before a single person stepped a foot on them."

"But why are they attacking me?" Gates queried.

Frank Osborne answered, "Because you have money. Or, more specifically, because your foundation has money. You heard Cassie just say they're a non-profit. But they still need money. They still need an income to pay for their operations. To pay salaries and office expenses, rent, travel, all their promotional costs, the printing and postage and air time, the server space for their blogs and everything like that. You'd be amazed at how much money some of those outfits go through. But because they're a non-profit, they don't really *earn* any money. They don't make any products. They don't provide any services. Their only way to get all the money they need is to ask for it. To raise donations. That makes them very aggressive. It makes them particularly aggressive with large foundations that give out the grants they rely upon. Of course, your foundation is the largest."

"We see that attitude a lot," Cassie Welch elaborated. "We see people who think they know very well how you should spend your money, and they're not afraid to pressure you into spending it exactly the way they think is right. That's all that stunt at Harvard was: a pressure play by the Habitat Defenders Fund. But we have ways to counteract them. That's a big part of what we do," said Welch. "We come up with strategies and programs to counteract and kind of neutralize the negative effects these pressure groups can have on your image and your public persona when they go after you. That's defensive practice rather than positive image building. We'd much rather do the offensive, you know, the positive image building over the defending against a negative image. But we're ready for it and we do it when we have to. We talked about all that, remember?. We said at the beginning of our relationship with you that there were some lingering, negative perceptions about you that we would have to overcome. Remember? We said at the time that those perceptions were mostly in the realm of business – in the business press and in inner circles where people worked in the software industry and the computer business and everything. We said at the time that since our aim was to build a broad-based, popular image, an image with the public at large, we didn't think those negative perceptions in the business world would hinder us too much. And they really haven't. I mean, I have to say that, to our credit, we've kept those lingering, kind-of negative perceptions sidelined and they haven't been a hindrance. I mean, our programs have really been very successful and I honestly thought that we were getting ready to wind down now. But now, of course, well, this whole thing has come up. It's too bad. But we're ready to deal with it. Again, dealing with attacks like this is a big part of what we do."

"Right," said Gates. "We went over all that and I know all the theory and I understand the difference between defensive programs and positive initiatives and all the rest. I don't need to hear all of that again now. Now we're dealing with specifics. We have this attack by the Habitat Defense Fund or the Defensive Fund or whatever they call themselves. And we have this whole image-dog idea that completely blew up in our face. Exactly what can we do about those problems? *Exactly* what?"

Welch and Osborne and Albert Wistol passed glances among themselves once again, a relay to assign the response. Cassie Welch spoke first.

"For starters, we think we should bring Peter Singer in," she said. "He came here before when we wanted him, when we said it was about philanthropy. He's got that new book out about philanthropy. He's writing articles about it. He was even in The Wall Street Journal. We think we should get him here and sit down with him and give him something good about the foundation, something fresh and new and maybe he'll come out with an article that will counteract some of this bad press."

"Who is he?" asked Gates.

"His name is Peter Singer," Frank Osborne answered. "We had him here once before for a meeting. He's one of the people we identified in our early research, when we were just getting started with you and we were researching to find independent voices we might bring over to our point of view. Who might, with a little bit of personal attention, give some independent credence to the image we've been building."

"He's a Princeton professor of something or other," Cassie Welch continued. "He writes a lot about philanthropy. That's why we thought he might be good to kind of, you know, win over. He's even got a new book out about it: The Life You Can Save. You've met him, Bill. He should come here again as long as he can talk to you directly. He's a bit of a sycophant that way.

All you have to do is meet with him, talk with him for a while, maybe have lunch with him. He'll be won over as long as he spends some time with you, Bill. After that, there's a good chance he'll give us some good press to counteract all this negative stuff."

"You just want to make sure it's an appropriate lunch," joined Albert Wistol boldly as he scanned his profile of Peter Singer stored on his laptop computer. As he spoke he stayed trained on the screen, daring not to glance upward at Gates or at Rin and Amanda joined close beside him. "The lunch should be modest, I mean," Wistol said. "Organic salads and things like that. Not a big smörgåsbord, that's for sure. He rails against excess. That's what it says in my profile here. He's all about animals, too. You know: animal rights. In fact, it says right here that his first public cause was animal rights. He was into that pretty heavily before he picked up philanthropy for a cause. That makes him really perfect for this ... for this ... for this ... you know, for this little crisis. I'd say he's the perfect guy for Bill to meet with right now."

"But why do I have to meet with him?" groused Gates. "Let's just have the foundation staff take care of that."

"That probably wouldn't work," explained Cassie Welch. "You have to meet with him personally so he'll feel like it's top-level. So he'll feel like *he's* top-level. You have to remember that being the wealthiest man in the world, being the leader of Microsoft, giving thirty-billion dollars to your own foundation, all that stuff carries an awful lot of weight. An awful lot. People feel awfully special if you pay attention to them. They feel important because you're important. Powerful, too."

"But this guy is a Princeton professor," said Gates.

"So what," said Welch. "Princeton professors want to feel important too – as long as they can think it's for the right reasons. That's where the foundation and all your philanthropy comes in. It gives them the right reason to like you. It gives you a lot of star power with people like this. We can put together the best program and create the best presentation and have the foundation staff tell him all about it. But nothing will stroke him like you spending personal time with him. You're Bill Gates."

"That's exactly why we identified him as a potential, independent ally at the start of this whole effort," explained Franklin Osborne. "That's one of the services we perform for you. We did a lot of research and picked him out as a person of influence who could possibly be enlisted to help build a positive public image for you. The fact that he's a Princeton professor, the fact that he writes books and articles all plays to our favor. Those things make him a person of influence. But we go beyond that with our research, because of course the world is full of people who have done this and done that. We also identify people who are personally susceptible because of their character, because of their needs, their psychological makeup and all that. There must be some stuff in that summary of Peter Singer that Al has right there that shows why we thought he'd fall in behind us. Why we thought he'd be a good person to recruit as a supporter. Isn't there, Al?"

"It says here that he distinguishes himself by being kind-of a saint or a martyr," Wistol read from the laptop. "In one interview I read for our research on him, he criticized himself for sometimes having a glass of wine or going to a concert or a movie instead of giving the money to a charity instead. He said that publicly He already gives a ton, but he knocked himself publicly for not giving more."

"You have to wonder why he doesn't just give it all away and go live in a cave some place," quipped Cassie Welch. "But of course, he'd never do that. That's one of the reasons why he's on our list. He really likes the notoriety. He likes all the fame and all the attention his views and his behavior bring him. He'd certainly like more personal attention from you, Bill. That's exactly why he's on our list. Because he's on a mission to enlighten all the rest of us, and because he really likes the attention and the notoriety that mission attracts for him. That kind of self-importance can make a person really useful to us. That's why we do so much research to find people like Peter Singer. If you win them over to your side, make them feel important and looked up to and everything, they can be a powerful mouthpiece. Peter Singer can be a very powerful mouthpiece for us, because, like Al said, he comes off like he's a saint or a martyr or something."

"Okay," said Gates. "I'll sit down with Peter Singer. Get him in here. Fly him in and put him up and I'll meet with him to talk about, well, to talk about what?"

"About the foundation, or course," answered Osborne. "It has to be about philanthropy. We'll come up with the specifics later. We can get together with the staff over there and come up with some kind of angle, some hook that hopefully will get him to give us some good press and counteract this little crisis, as Al just called it."

"But that's only one thing," said Gates. "What else can we do, because we have to do more than just that."

Osborne, Wistol and Welch shot round their glances again.

"Well of course we plan to do more," replied Osborne. "But, as we said at the start of this meeting, we're still assessing the situation and putting a full plan fully together. We just haven't had time. I mean, this whole thing just happened. This meeting was considered preliminary, a first step."

"I can assess the situation for you," squabbed Gates. "The situation is terrible. We're looking at failure. A big failure. The image dog may not have been our biggest initiative, but it was supposed to help create a positive image. Instead it's done exactly the opposite. It's created a negative image. They're calling me a fraud. That's my definition of failure. We need a plan right away – first, to prevent this from getting any worse, and second, to undo the damage. That's my assessment: failure. We need to change that right now."

"Right. But, well, at least we can say, I mean, this isn't exactly good news, but I think that at least we've seen the worst of it," Osborne ventured. "I don't expect it to get any worse now, and in fact, based on the usual patterns these things follow, we could say it's come to a head now and it should start to decline. I mean, after David Letterman did that bit on his show last night . . .."

"You mean his 'ten reasons why Bill Gates owns a dog,'" Gates shot in.

"Right, right," Osborne nodded in a feint to disguise his hesitation.

"I sure hope that's the peak. I don't see how it can get any worse after that," said Gates derisively.

"We're coming up with some responses right now," rushed out Cassie Welch. "We haven't had time to finalize anything yet, like Franklin just said. But we're close to having some more programs, some placements and things like that to help neutralize this. Like the meeting with Peter Singer. That's a really good start. It could lead to a high-level placement for us, something very complimentary in one of the big national papers, the Times or the Wall Street Journal or something. So we're already on top of that, and we'll have other things too, real soon. Maybe even by tomorrow. Or in a day or two. Just as soon as we finish some research and can run down some leads and everything. In the meantime, the best thing to do is just stay with the program. Don't let them rattle you. Just hold on and stay with the program as a way to show everyone they're wrong."

"You mean I should keep Rin around?" quizzed Gates.

"Definitely," Welch replied.

He turned his head and glanced once again thoughtfully at Rin beside him. He saw Amanda too, perked in her position beside Rin.

"But it didn't work," said Gates. "We had him here for one very specific reason and now that reason no longer applies. Keeping him now would be a bad business decision. Even if, like you said, by having him around it would help neutralize the damage, it still wouldn't do anything to build a positive image. That was our goal: to use him to somehow subtly tie me to the idea of the easy-going entrepreneur, the unconventional tech-innovator and all that. We're past that now. It can't work anymore. Not after all this has come out. Even if we undo the damage, we can't use Rin the way we first planned. Keeping him around would be a bad business decision."

Amanda stood up abruptly. On her feet she looked more imposing than she had in her quiet sequester half behind Bill Gates. She stood on alert, piqued and keenly observant. Could Rin really now vanish, she worried. Would these people have the ill-sense to actually banish him? She turned her head and looked backward at Macklam against the wall. She glanced at Gates. She gazed round pointedly at Melinda Gates, at Osborne, Welch and at Albert Wistol. Only Wistol did not look back at her. His focus stayed down at the computer screen in front of him. Uncertainty vexed his expression. Is he the one who will break, Amanda wondered. In their conversations, Rin had told her about the people he met keeping time with Bill Gates. He had mentioned one who was fearful and easily bent. Wistol is the one, she concluded.

When Welch, Wistol and Franklin Osborne exchanged looks once again, Cassie Welch saw dread and anxiety cross Albert Wistol's face.

Raising her head higher, Amanda stepped in his direction.

"Hey," snapped Gates. "Sit down."

Amanda swung a glance at Gates. She stretched farther and looked at Rin still seated beside him. She bowed her head reluctantly and obeyed. But now she sat a step ahead of Rin, nearer the table than she was before.

Osborne said, "Well, of course, Bill, the ultimate decision about ending the program is all up to you."

"I guess that means we'll have to say goodbye to you too, right Reggie?" Cassie Welch said to Reginald Macklam at his position along the wall.

"That's a final decision that's up to Bill, too. Or I should say, it's up to Bill and Melinda," Macklam replied. "Let's not forget that there's still young Amanda here. And those other fellows, too. We still have their breeding to see to. That is, if you're still interested, Mrs. Gates."

"Of course I'm still interested," Melinda replied. "I definitely want to get that done. I'm committed to it."

"Because, you see," said Macklam, "we're getting close to the time when Amanda is ready. You have to remember that there's a biological deadline we're facing. She'll need to have a husband when that deadline arrives. She's not too far away from it now."

Abruptly Amanda stood up again.

"You see," chuckled Macklam. "I think she knows it too."

"I said sit down," Gates snapped at her, but Amanda remained on her feet.

"Maybe she's even closer than I imagined," Macklam mused half to himself.

"Sit down," Gates insisted more stridently, but still Amanda stayed upright. Wistol no longer could keep his stare focused on the laptop. He looked up at her with alarm. Seeing his expression, Amanda took a step toward him.

"Hey," said Gates. "I told you to sit down."

Macklam began to rise from his chair to intercept her. But before the trainer was fully up, Rin stood and stepped forward. Without uttering a word Rin herded Amanda gently back to sit beside him again, off the elbow of Bill Gates.

"Wow," marveled Cassie Welch. "He really does fit right in with you, Bill. It's like he knows exactly what you want."

Macklam said, "We can see what Amanda wants. It looks to me like she's just about ready to go. If you still want to select the best partner for her,

Mrs. Gates, you really should do it right away."

"I can see that," Melinda said. "It's just been so tough to get to it. And, to tell you the truth, I'm just not too thrilled about the choices. I'm not too thrilled with those four boys you've got down there. I read the report you sent me about them. I read part of it, I mean. It's hard to get motivated because I'm just not too excited about what I see."

"But they're all you have to choose from right now," Macklam said. "Maybe if you come down and do some observing yourself, you'll feel differently. That was the original plan, you'll remember. The plan was that you'd come down yourself and check them out and see which one has the best disposition. We'd do some observing ourselves, Debbie Green and I. And we'd do those quick little daily summaries for you to look at. That was the original plan, and we've been doing that religiously, Mrs. Gates. But unless you go over those reports, and unless you spend some time down there with the boys themselves . . .."

"Oh, I know," said Melinda. "When we started I expected to have so much more time. I'm just so busy now. But still, I feel that if I just had some better choices down there . . .."

"It's funny," chuckled Macklam, "I mean, it's too late now, but Debbie and I felt from the start that Gandhi would have made a good partner for her, if he had stayed around."

"Gandhi *would* be a good partner," returned Melinda Gates. "I wish we had kept him. He's the one who reminded me so much of my own Aussies when I was a little girl. Where is he now, Reggie? Do you think we can get him back?"

"Get him back?" Macklam quandaried in surprise. "You'd want to get him back? Now?"

"Why not? Yes, of course I would. We have a little more time, don't we? If you could get him right away, I'd still be able to have a quick look and then make a final decision."

"But I don't know where he is," replied Macklam. "He was sold."

"But you could find out who bought him. You could buy him back."

"But I'd have to do it right away."

She merely looked back at him in reply.

"But you'd still come down and review them all?" Macklam asked her.

"Yes. As a final check. I mean, we'd want to be sure."

"Then let me make sure I have all my instructions straight," said Macklam. "First I find Gandhi and get him back down there. Then, Mrs. Gates, you'll come down right away and make a selection. You'll choose one of the five. And then we'll have our nuptials for Amanda here."

"That's right," she said.

"And, Bill, you want me to get rid of Rin?"

Gates swiveled his head and looked at Rin sitting dutifully at ease near his side.

"He looks awfully comfortable to me," ventured Cassie Welch. "He looks to me like he's right where he belongs."

"Yeah," said Gates, almost bemused. "A lot of times now I almost forget he's around."

"You see," said Welch. "He's really no trouble at all. He really is right where he belongs. If he was mine I'd sure want to keep him around."

"But we brought him here for a reason, and now that reason no longer applies."

"So what," said Welch. "You could still keep him around. Just for yourself. Just for the friendship. Look at him, Bill. Hasn't he been a really good friend for you?"

Gates gazed thoughtfully at Rin.

"I don't know," he said. "I never stopped to think about it."

"But you can see it right now just by looking at him."

"Maybe. But this is business," said Gates. "The program is over. The whole thing's been exposed. There's just no reason to keep him around. It would be a bad business decision."

"Well, I just think it's a shame," Welch said.

"It would be a bad business decision," Gates repeated. "He's got to go."

Spontaneously Amanda shot to her feet. Not waiting to be corralled this time, she bounded unhesitantly toward Wistol's seat at the table. Rin was up and after her at once, starting half a leap behind her but pulling even with her in his second stride. But this time he could not stop her. With both Rin and Amanda now crashing towards him, Wistol sprang out of his chair, flipping it backward behind him so it whumped on the floor. Throwing out his hands awkwardly in panic and fright, he whacked the open screen of his laptop, so that the computer spun around a turn on the table, exposing the screen for the others to see. Wistol had been staring at the word *calm* superimposed on an animation of gently breaking waves.

What a sorry cliché, thought Cassie Welch, who nevertheless stood up very quickly to intercept both Rin and Amanda by opening wide her arms. She blocked them just before they reached Albert Wistol, who had abandoned the table and was striding away rapidly in retreat. He reached the conference room door and glanced back very quickly before wedging it open and sliding sidelong through the gap to safety.

"This is absolutely ridiculous," Gates erupted. "How can we have a meeting here when he loses control at the smallest little thing. Frank, get someone else for that job," Gates commanded with a head gesture toward the space where Wistol had sat. "I'm sure you can find someone else who can read to us about Peter Singer or whoever just as well as he can. And Reggie, get those two out of here now. I don't want any more interruptions. We need to talk a lot more about what we're going to do to fix all this."

CHAPTER 15

Dremmel and Blake stood shoulder to shoulder outside in their yard, peering across Amanda's spacious lot toward the two deserted yards that stood beyond hers. Amanda was not around, but they figured she was simply inside her home. Rin, on the other hand, had vanished, leaving the fourth yard and its attached house, the ones on the opposite end of the complex, now fully vacant.

"I wonder if someone else is going to move in there now," Dremmel mused.

"Who knows," said Blake. "I sure wouldn't want to live there. Look at how small it is."

"I wouldn't want to live there either," Dremmel agreed. "Especially not after living here. But there's one thing you have to remember, though: compared to a lot of other places it's really not that bad over there. It only looks bad to us now because we're used to all this. I don't ever want to leave this."

"When do you think Big Gandhi will get here?"

"I don't know for sure," Dremmel answered. "It's going to be soon. Very soon. We know that for sure because Debbie Green told us that

Macklam is going to get him right now. The only thing I'm not completely sure about is how long that will take. Maybe tomorrow. Maybe even today. Maybe in just a little while. I don't know for sure. But I can tell you this: I'll be awfully glad to see him when he gets here."

"Me too," Blake said. "I'll be really glad too. I never would have told you this before, but I wasn't too excited about it when you first said he was coming back. But now I can't wait. Just like you."

"Why didn't you want him to come back?" Dremmel asked.

"'Cause Amanda was going for me back then. That's how it looked to me. She talked to me all the time. It's like every time I was around she wanted to be with me. I thought for sure I'd get to marry her and then I'd be all right. I'd get to stay here. I didn't need Big Gandhi. That's how it looked back then – back when you first told us he was coming back. Heck, I thought that, if anything, he'd just get in the way. But now she won't even look at me."

"Now she doesn't look at anyone," Dremmel said.

"I know," said Blake. "It's not like it's anything that *I've* done. It's more like, she's the one who changed. She's just different now."

"She's very, very different," Dremmel agreed. "I never thought this would happen. I wasn't so sure she would marry you. I mean, I wasn't as sure as you say you were. But I never thought she'd go for that nonnie over us. Not over any of us. Not even Web. Now that nonnie's not even here anymore. Rin disappeared just like I said he would. But now she's even worse. You'd think she would come around after Rin disappeared. I mean, it's as clear as can be, just like I told her. That kind always just vanishes. It could happen to her. She could lose this big beautiful house of hers. But all she wants now is him. All the sudden she doesn't want anything to do with us. She won't even talk to us."

"She'll get hers," said Blake. "I can't believe I wasted my time on her."

"You were doing it for her," said Dremmel. "We didn't want to see her go over to that side. We didn't want to see her give everything up. But now she's doing exactly that."

"I wonder what Big Gandhi will say about her," Blake mused.

"He'll say she's an idiot," answered Dremmel. "Especially if she turns him down, too. I mean, she could choose Big Gandhi. That would be okay. That would be just perfect. But the way she's going now, I don't think she'll even want to have anything to do with him."

"Do you think he'll like her?" Blake asked. "I mean, do you think he'd want to marry her?"

"Not if she's like this."

"Do you think he'll like us?" asked Blake.

"Of course he will. We're the whole reason he's coming back here."

"Debbie Green doesn't like me very much," Blake confessed in a hung tone.

"What do you mean?" Dremmel asked him.

"Remember when we first heard them talking? When we heard Macklam and Debbie Green talking over on their side of the wall and we first heard them say Big Gandhi is coming back?"

"Of course I remember," said Dremmel with sudden caution and a dash of simmering irritation.

"Well, it wasn't just you they were talking about. Before they got to Big Gandhi, I mean. They were talking about all of us. That was before I woke you up. Web and Georgie – they thought they were okay. But they didn't have many good things to say about you. They didn't have many good things to say about me, either. That's when I went to wake you up. They said you were nervous and jumpy. That part's still true. But they didn't think very much of me, either. They said I just goof around all the time. That I'm always just running and jumping and things like that. They said that's not too smart. They said Georgie and Web were smarter than me. Smarter than you, too."

"They said Georgie and Web are smarter than me?"

"Yeah. They said Georgie and Web are the two leaders around here. They said they're the ones who call the shots."

"That's ridiculous," Dremmel complained.

"I'm just telling you what they said."

"Georgie and Web?"

"Yep. Georgie and Web."

"Debbie Green said that, too?"

"Debbie Green said the most of it," Blake answered.

"I really can't believe that. I mean, Macklam, I can see. He's hardly ever around. He was backing that Rin. He spent all of his time with him. And now we see where that's got him. But Debbie Green! She's around here all the time. She sees what goes on. How could she ever think Georgie and Web are smarter than me?"

"I'm just telling you what I heard."

"Man, I'll be glad when Big Gandhi gets here."

"Me too," said Blake. "Do you think he'll like Georgie and Web more than us? Will he think they're smarter?"

"Of course not. He'll be right here with us. How could he ever think that?"

"Hey, who's that over there?" Blake asked in a sudden turn. In the fourth yard, two places beyond Amanda's spacious lot, they saw another fellow standing in Rin's old spot, regarding them with an expression they could not decipher.

"Holy cow," said Dremmel. "I don't know who that is. He made me jump. For a second I thought it was Rin. But it's definitely not Rin. No way."

"Rin is gone and he's not coming back. But who do you think that is?"

"I don't know. Maybe it's another nonnie."

"But he looks like one of us. He looks like he has breeding."

"Sometimes they they just look that way," said Dremmel. "You can't always go by looks. Sometimes they look just like us. But I think he's a non-breed."

"You don't think he's Big Gandhi, do you?" Blake wondered. "You just said he might get here later today."

"He's not Big Gandhi. No way. Big Gandhi wouldn't be over there. Not in that little place where Rin used to live. That's the place for non-breeds."

"But where else will Big Gandhi go?"

"I don't know," answered Dremmel. "I never really thought about it. But I know he won't go there."

"Then where?"

"I don't know. Maybe he'll go in the place right next to Amanda's. The one that's a little closer to us. That one's not very nice either, but at least it's not as bad as that place on the end. That one's for nonnies."

"Are you Big Gandhi?" Blake called across.

"Shhh," hissed Dremmel.

But the newcomer had heard.

"Big Gandhi? *Big* Gandhi? Who's that?" the stranger called back. "I don't know anyone named Big Gandhi."

"You see," Dremmel tossed to Blake. "I told you he's not Big Gandhi."

"My name is Gandhi," said the new guy. "I don't know any Big Gandhis. Unless you mean my father. But his name wasn't Big Gandhi either."

"It must be him," Blake said in a concealing tone to Dremmel.

"But he just said he's not Big Gandhi."

"But he's *Gandhi*," Blake countered. "He must be the same one. He just doesn't say *Big*. That's all. We've heard Macklam call him that – call him just Gandhi, I mean. Debbie Green, too. Sometimes she just calls him Gandhi too."

"But they can talk like that. They're different than us. They can say a lot of things different than we do."

"But so can he if he's really Big Gandhi. Gandhi, I mean. Big Gandhi can talk the same as them."

"Ask him if he used to live here before," Dremmel said to Blake.

Blake called across, "Are you the one who used to live here? The one who used to live here and the one who's coming back now?"

"I lived here once. But only for a little while. And I didn't know anything about coming back. This whole thing's a surprise to me. This place is different too. A lot different. When I was here there was just one home, that one over there where you guys are now. That was the only home and your yard was the only yard. Who are you guys, anyway?"

"My name is Blake and this here is Dremmel. We've been waiting for you."

"You've been waiting for me? Why are you waiting for me?"

"Because we have breeding, just like you. We've been waiting for you so that all of us with breeding can all stay here together and we won't be sent away. All of us except Amanda, I mean."

"Amanda? Who's Amanda?" Gandhi asked.

"She lives in this big house right here," Blake answered. "We were supposed to marry her. One of us was, I mean. Then it turned out that you were coming and we kind of thought that you would be the one who would marry her. But now the whole thing has changed. We don't even know if you'd want to marry her now."

"Marry her? I don't even know who she is."

"I'm Amanda," the lady announced as she strode out her door, drawn by their back-and-forth queries and calls. She shone from the full ripening that had seized her suddenly. It now spread daring radiance through all of her mien. "I heard these two talking about me when I was inside. Are you Big Gandhi?"

"My name is just Gandhi."

"Oh." She smiled. "I like that better."

"Were you waiting for me too?"

"No," she said. "I'm not waiting for anybody."

"It's probably best if you don't even talk to her," Blake said to Gandhi.

"Shhh," Dremmel rushed aside to Blake. "Don't say that to him."

"Why not?"

"He can figure it out for himself."

Gandhi asked Amanda, "then you just live here all by yourself?"

"I do now," she said.

"What do you mean by 'now'? Was someone else here with you before?"

"There was someone over there, in your house. His name is Rin."

"He's a non-breed," Blake interjected. "But now he's gone. We don't have to worry about him at all anymore."

"Were you going to get married to Rin?" Gandhi asked Amanda.

"That was never anyone's plan. Except mine."

"You see," said Blake. "It's like I said: it's best if you don't even talk to her."

"You guys should just be quiet," Gandhi said to Dremmel and Blake.

"But this Rin that she likes is a nonnie," Dremmel said with emphatic restraint. "We tried to warn her about him. I told her a hundred times she has to stick to her own kind. I told her he doesn't have breeding. He doesn't have anything. Not a thing. I told her he'll only just disappear. And now he did. He's gone. And she still doesn't listen to me."

"When did he leave?" Gandhi asked Amanda.

"A couple of days ago."

"Oh," he said. "I'm sorry."

"What!" Dremmel blurted. "You're sorry? But he was just a nonnie. Everybody knew he was going to go. Now we know she's going to go too."

"That's right about when I left," Gandhi continued with Amanda. "A couple of days ago I was in a big house near some woods, with a big yard that had lots of shade. The house had a lot of nice rooms that were on different levels so there were a lot of neat little places inside, little nooks and pockets and places like that. I had a family there too. With two kids. Two older kids. Teenagers. They liked to hike around a lot and we'd go out in the woods all the time. We'd climb things together, up rocks and steep slopes. They really loved to climb and so I got pretty good at it too. Sometimes they'd like to just sit and talk to me, too. We spent all our time together. But then all the sudden I was gone."

"But that's because you're supposed to come back here," said Dremmel.

"But coming back here means leaving there. I'd much rather be back there."

"But this is the best place ever," said Blake.

"You just said yourself it's even better here now," Dremmel added. "You said it's nicer now than the first time you were here."

"But I liked it better where I was," said Gandhi.

Dremmel stood agape, while Blake retorted, "But Bill Gates wanted you to come back here."

"No kidding," said Gandhi. "I'm sure that's why I'm here. But I didn't want to come back."

"But now you get to be Bill Gates' dog," Blake struggled to explain.

"I was Bill Gates' dog the last time I was here. For a little while, anyway. It ended pretty quickly but I didn't mind. He never treated me very nice."

"Rin was Bill Gates' dog," Amanda said. "He told me that for a while

Bill Gates didn't treat him very nice, either. But then it got better, Rin said. He said that after a while it just seemed like he belonged there. He said it seemed almost like he'd always been there. After a while, he said, he started to like Bill Gates."

"That's why she wanted to marry him," bleated Blake. "Because he was Bill Gates' dog."

"I want to marry him still, and he's not Bill Gates' dog anymore," she said in quiet retort.

"That's right," Blake sneered. "He's nothing anymore. He's gone."

"I wish I was gone too," said Amanda.

"You're going to be," Blake taunted. "You just wait and see."

"If I could only get out of here, I'd go find him," she said.

"But how would you find him?" asked Gandhi. "Have you ever been out there? It's so big. How would you know where to go? There's so many places he could be. And even if you knew where he was, how could you figure out how to get there? It's so big out there, and there's so many places."

"I've been out there a little, with Rin and with Macklam. Macklam took us places sometimes. And sometimes he just took us for long walks around here. So I know what it's like out there. I know how big it is. I don't care. I'd just keep going until I found Rin."

"Macklam used to take me out a lot too," said Gandhi.

"But this is the best place I've ever seen," Dremmel whined.

"When I lived here the first time Macklam made things a lot easier for me," Gandhi explained to Amanda. "I'm glad he's still around here now. But I still wish I was back home, back at the home where they took me from."

Amanda asked him, "If you liked it there so much, wasn't there anything you could have done to stay there?"

"I don't know. I never thought to try. I never thought that I would have to do anything, because I never knew that I'd be taken away. I mean, if I stopped to think about it I knew that sooner or later it would end. We all know that. But it's not like there was a date written on the calendar that I could plan for or anything. It just happened without any notice or warning or anything. Everything was normal. Everything was going along the same as always. Then all of the sudden a couple of days ago it ended. I was gone. How could I try to stop something if I didn't know it was coming?"

"I don't know," said Amanda. "It just seems like it's better to try. It's better to do something than it is to just sit. Don't you think?"

"Yeah, yeah, I guess you're right. I guess it would be better to do something. But what?"

Amanda couldn't answer. But when she returned to the solitude of her house, she felt impelling passion push her irresistibly now toward some resolute action. She had to do something. Something! Her destiny now was attached to the wandering Rin. After the discussion with Gandhi outside, she felt a stronger, new surge of the sauntering restlessness that had ruled her since Rin's banishment. Alone inside her home, she fretted and she paced as she cursed the confinement that bottled all the kinetic, soaring impulses now driving her outward toward him. So that when Debbie Green walked suddenly in through the door, Amanda spontaneously rushed the opening. She brushed instantly past the startled Green, wriggling through the door before it closed and gaining the big outer room that Green kept so disordered. Amanda cleared the work room in bounds. She hit the exit handle to burst out of the building's main door and she ran joyously into the big air beyond.

Amanda made for the hill that stood on the back side of the compound, around the building and around their fenced-in yards. She crested the knoll with furious speed and sprinted down the back to find the familiar trail that ran into the woods. Debbie Green let out yells and exclamations before finally dashing herself through Amanda's door and then bursting outside and pushing up the hill in a hopeless chase to catch Amanda.

Gandhi had gone inside his house before all that happened, so he missed the spectacle. But Dremmel and Blake had remained outside in their yard after the encounter with Amanda and Gandhi had ended. They witnessed Amanda's flight. Now suddenly gaping, instantly astonished, struck into startled silence, they watched Amanda's jubilant dash outside their fenced lots and beyond the close bounds of their compound. Their stare followed her up the knoll till she disappeared over its crest. They watched Debbie Green rumble up the hill after her, shouting to Amanda, flagging from fatigue and groaning a futile protest as she paused only briefly at the top, before starting down toward the woods and disappearing from their sight.

CHAPTER 16

At the same time, inside their house, Georgie and Web were locked in an urgent negotiation.

"I just don't think it's the right time, Georgie," stressed Web. "Everything's different now. It's not the same as it was when we first talked about this. Now Big Gandhi is coming. Debbie Green told us for sure that Macklam is going to get him. It's not the same as it was, Georgie. I don't think you should do it now."

"I know it's not the same as it was," replied Georgie with equal vigor. "And that's exactly why I have to go right now. Right now in the broad daylight. Once Gandhi gets here, who knows if I'll ever get the chance. Who knows what it'll be like then. I gotta go right now, Web. Don't you see? This might be my only chance. It's all set up now and everything. With just a little help from you, I can get out of here and go to Amanda's and be back before anybody ever knows I'm gone. And, hey, Web, besides, have you seen Amanda lately? Did you see her this morning? Did you see how good she's lookin'? I mean, how can a guy resist? Come on, Web. I can't wait. I gotta go now."

"But Amanda turned against us," Web said. "All she wants now is Rin.

Dremmel said she's probably gonna go away for that. She's probably gonna vanish."

"No kidding," Georgie answered. "But that's another reason why I gotta go now, Web. Right now. Before she's gone. There's no time to wait. And look, Web. Look at the vacuum cleaner right there. It's right there where Debbie Green left it. Just like I said she would. In my room and everything. Just like I said she would leave it sooner or later. It's an invitation, Web, don't you see? It's like an open invitation. I can get to Amanda now before she's gone. I can get there before Big Gandhi gets here. Come on, Web. I can feel it so strong I can taste it."

"But if Dremmel finds out ... ."

"Dremmel won't find out. How could he? He's outside waiting for Big Gandhi with Blake. Those two will be out there all day. And Amanda's just been moping around inside her house. I can get in and get her now and they'll never know what's going on. It's the perfect time, Web. There'll never be a better time than right now."

"It's too risky, Georgie."

"It's not risky at all, Web. That's what makes it so perfect. All you gotta do is hold the cleaner there tight in the corner, like we talked about before. Come on, Web. I wouldn't even ask ya if I didn't really, really need your help. I tried jumping on it just a minute ago, just for the heck of it, just to try, but its wheels kicked it away from the wall, just like before. You just gotta hold it in place. Wedge it up against the wall there real hard and just hold it so I can jump on it and then just spring up over the wall. Come on, Web. You told me before that you'd help me. You can't go back on it now."

"But what if Debbie Green's out there?"

"She's not out there, Web. We both just heard her go out."

"But she yelled something, too," said Web. "It sounded like something was wrong. What if something was wrong and she comes right back?"

"There wasn't anything wrong, Web. We always hear her rushing around and stumbling around out there. Who knows why. It doesn't mean something's wrong. But, come on, Web. I really gotta go now. Before she comes back. Now while Amanda's still here. I can't stop thinkin' about her, Web. The way that she looks. Come on. You said you'd help me. I was counting on you, Web. You can't back down on me now."

"But how can you be so sure you'll be back before Debbie Green gets back?"

"I'm just sure. I'm very sure. I told you, I'm just gonna be gone a little while. I'll be there and back before anyone knows. You said you'd help me, Web. You gotta do it now."

"I don't know, Georgie. Now things are different. Now it's . . ., it's . . .."

"Come on, Web. You promised me."

"I did?"

"Yes, you did."

"I said the word *promise*?"

"You said you promised you'd help me get over."

While Web leaned all of his body weight powerfully to wedge the big canister securely against the wall, Georgie backed away three paces to gain a running start.

"Now, remember, Web," Georgie said, "I can let myself back in. The door handle works from Debbie Green's side. It's only from in here you can't turn it. So I'll get back in on my own. You don't have to do anything after this. Just go outside and stay with Dremmel and Blake. Tell them I'm in here taking a nap or something. When I come back I'll go out there too. Then you'll know it's okay."

With that Georgie kicked into a run and, bursting onto the top of the platform – which Web held steady with his body's full weight – Georgie leaped up vigorously over the cropped height of the partition wall.

CHAPTER 17

Web walked outside to find Dremmel and Blake staring silently out through the fence at the route over which Amanda and then Debbie Green had just raced and then dropped out of sight. Web approached them from behind. He waited for them to recognize him with a comment or at least a nod. But Dremmel and Blake dumbly peered out unaware that Web had approached them at all. After a pause Web said, "hey, guys, what are ya doin'? I was just inside. Georgie is taking a nap. I just thought I'd come out on my own and see what you're doin'."

"Amanda just ran away," said Blake without turning to face him.

"What? Amanda ran away? She ran inside, you mean? Amanda's inside her house. Isn't she?"

"Not anymore," said Dremmel, who, like Blake, stared intensely out at the knoll. "She just took off. We saw her. We saw her run off over that little hill right there. She went over the top and that's the last we saw of her. Debbie Green went after her. That's the last we saw of her, too."

"No," said Web.

"We just saw her," insisted Dremmel.

"How could she get out?"

"How the hell do we know how she got out," snapped Blake. "We didn't see her get out. We saw her run over the hill."

"Then who's in her house?" queried Web.

"Damn it, Web. No one's in her house," Blake slapped back. "We just told you that. She just ran away. We saw her just run away just now."

"Are you sure about that?"

"Yes, Web. We're sure," answered Dremmel. "We just saw her. Both of us just saw her."

"So she's not in her house?"

"No, Web. She's not in her house."

"Oh no," peeped Web.

"I'll say oh no," Blake volleyed. "She really did it to herself this time."

Web stepped up to join their rank, so that the three of them stood shoulder to shoulder gazing far outside their enclosure.

"Where did she go?" asked Web.

"How in the hell should we know," sneered Blake. "She didn't tell us. She barely even talked to us anymore."

"She's just getting out," said Dremmel, half to himself. "She's going away, that's all. She knew what was coming. She knew she was going out anyway. She knew she was going to vanish. Maybe this was her way to try to stop it. That would be just like her: to run away so she wouldn't get taken away. To do it herself, kind of. Although I don't see what this is going to get her. She's still gone. She's still not here, any way you look at it."

"Maybe she's going after that damn Rin," Blake said with loathing.

"Rin's gone," answered Dremmel. "He's gone and he's not coming back and nobody knows where he is anymore. She doesn't know where he is. She can't be going after Rin if she doesn't know where he is."

"She thinks she knows everything," said Blake.

"She knew she was going to disappear. She was right about that much at least. But anyone could see that."

"When is she coming back?" Web asked.

Annoyed at the question, Blake turned his head to glance at Web and mock him with his glare. But in the movement, as his eyes brushed over the kennel building, Blake noticed someone looking out from Amanda's back door.

"Who's that?" he said startled.

"Who's what?" Dremmel bounced.

"Who's where?" asked Web, shot instantly with dread.

"I just saw someone in Amanda's house," said Blake.

"Not in Amanda's house," Web argued.

"Yes, in Amanda's house. I just saw them right there in the door. They were looking out. When I turned around they jumped back in real fast, but not before I saw them."

"Who was it?" asked Dremmel.

"I don't think it was anyone," said Web.

"I don't know who it was," answered Blake. "I didn't see them clearly enough. But I know I saw someone. They were there looking out right when I turned around."

"It must have been Big Gandhi," Dremmel said.

"Big Gandhi?" Web echoed desperately. "We're still waiting for Big Gandhi, right guys? That's why we're out here, right? Because we're waiting for Big Gandhi."

"I don't think it was Gandhi," Blake replied.

"Why not?" asked Dremmel.

"I don't know. It just didn't look like Big Gandhi to me. Besides, how would he get into Amanda's house? We saw him go into his own place, his place on the end, just a little while ago. He couldn't get into Amanda's from there."

"Maybe it was his place you saw," Dremmel reasoned. "Maybe you saw Big Gandhi looking out his own door and you just thought it was Amanda's door."

"But we're still waiting for Big Gandhi," Web interrupted. "When do you think he'll get here?"

"No," said Blake. "I know what I saw. It was definitely Amanda's house and there was definitely someone looking out the door."

"When do you think Big Gandhi will get here?" Web went on.

"Would you shut up," snapped Blake. "Big Gandhi is already here. We were talking to him when you were inside just now."

"You were? You were talking to Big Gandhi?"

Dremmel said, "Well we know it can't be Amanda. We just saw Amanda take off. There's no doubt about that. We saw Debbie Green go right after her, too."

"What did Big Gandhi say?" Web continued.

"Come on, Web," said Dremmel. "We're trying to figure this out. If Blake really saw somebody inside Amanda's house, but if we're all right here, who could it be?"

"Hey, wait a minute," said Blake. "Where's Georgie?"

"Web said he's inside sleeping."

Both Dremmel and Blake turned admonishing gazes to Web.

"That's what he told me," Web said defensively.

"You idiot," Blake said. "I'm going over there to find out myself."

As Blake hustled across the yard to the edge of the building, Dremmel, then Web, followed close behind him.

"Hey," Blake called toward Amanda's door. "Hey. Who's in there? Georgie, is that you in there?"

With reluctant steps, feeling uncharacteristically hesitant, Georgie came out of the door.

"I don't believe this," Dremmel shouted. "Georgie, what in the hell are you doing over there!"

"I came over to see Amanda," said Georgie defensively. "I just wanted to see her. Honest. I just wanted to talk to her. I figured it was time one of us talk to her."

"You're going to wreck everything," groaned Dremmel. "You're going to get us all in trouble."

"How in the hell did you get over there?" Blake demanded.

"I went over the wall in my room. The half wall. Web held the cleaner so I could jump on it like a platform and I jumped up over the wall. Then I just let myself in here."

"Well you'd better get back here right now," insisted Dremmel. "I mean right now. Right now. Before someone comes."

"But I can't get out," answered Georgie. "That's the problem. That's the one part I didn't think of. I can't open Amanda's door from the inside. It's like ours. You can open it from Debbie Green's room to get in here. But it has that different handle inside. Just like ours. I can't open it. I can't let myself out."

"Oh my God," Dremmel moaned. "I don't believe this."

"But you guys can let me out," said Georgie. "That's why I came out here just now. I'm sorry I have to ask. I mean, I'm sorry I have to bother you, but you hafta let me out."

"How can *we* let you out," Dremmel whined.

"Blake, you can jump real high," said Georgie. "Just come over the wall like I did. Web has to help you. He'll show you how. Just jump over the wall like I did. Once you're in Debbie Green's room you can come over here and open the door from that side. You can open the door and let me out and then we can both get back in there through our own door."

"I can get over that wall with no problem," said Blake.

"Then come right away," Georgie urged. "Do it right now, before someone comes."

"Oh no he doesn't," ordered Dremmel. "He's not going over there too. That will only make it worse."

"But he's got to," Georgie pleaded. "Come on, Blake. You can get over here and open the door and we'll be back before anybody knows we were gone. No one will ever know."

"I can clear that wall no problem," said Blake. He turned and started toward the house in a strut.

"Then wait a minute," said Dremmel. "If you're going, then I'm going too. There's no way I'm going to leave this for you two guys to screw up. No way at all am I going to let you guys out there alone. I'm going too and then we're all coming right back."

Web held the platform from slipping while Dremmel and Blake bounded over. Then he gazed around with sudden comprehension: he was alone. Web walked out into the yard to try to look into Amanda's home to spy the others.

On the other side of the wall, Blake plunged down the door handle assertively and pushed open the door to Amanda's home. Dremmel brushed past him to enter, stepping into the room and stopping face-on with Georgie where he waited for them.

"Stay there and hold the door," Dremmel shot backward to Blake. "Don't let it close whatever you do. If it closes we'll all be trapped in here."

"Just get out here," groused Blake. "I don't want to stand here holding the door for you."

"We're coming," said Dremmel. "I just want to look around once real fast."

"Look around!" Blake exclaimed. "Why do you get to look around? I don't want to stand here holding the door for you while you look around."

"Just wait," said Dremmel. He looked at Georgie. "This is the dumbest thing you could have ever done," Dremmel said to him.

"I just wanted to talk to her, Dremmel. That's all. You know: just to set her straight. But Dremmel, listen to this. She's not here. Amanda is gone. She's not anywhere inside here and we know she's not outside either. She disappeared. Amanda vanished just like you said she would, without any warning or anything like that."

"She didn't just disappear, you idiot. She ran away. Blake and I saw her. When you were breaking in or breaking out or whatever it is you did, we saw her run away outside."

"No you didn't," said Georgie.

"Hey you guys. Come on," Blake called. "I don't want to be stuck here holding this door."

"Yes we did," Dremmel said to Georgie. "When we were outside just now we both saw her run off. We watched her all the way until she went out of sight. Then we watched Debbie Green chasing her. We saw the whole thing."

"Where?" Georgie asked suddenly piqued.

"Right out here," said Dremmel. He led Georgie through Amanda's place to the back door that let out to her yard.

"Hey," Blake shouted. "Hey. Get back here right now. I'm not going to just stand here holding this door for you!"

"Just a second," Dremmel yelled back. To Georgie he said, "See? Come out here and look. See that little hill over there? She went up right up over the top and straight down the other side. She just kept on going as fast as she could. That's the last we saw of her."

"So she's all alone out there?" asked Georgie with growing interest.

"She must be," said Dremmel. "Debbie Green was chasing her but there's no way she was going to catch her. Macklam could get her, but there's no way Debbie Green is ever going to run her down."

"What do you think she's doing out there?" wondered Georgie.

"She's running away. Or maybe she's just hiding by now."

"She must be in the woods or something."

"I guess so," said Dremmel. "Wherever she is, she's not coming back. I know we're never going to see her again."

"Hey you guys," shouted Blake through the house from the door he held open. "I'm not going to wait here another second. You'd better get out here right now."

"Okay, okay, we're coming," yelled Dremmel. But as they re-entered the home to return to Blake, Georgie spun his head backward to peer across the yard at the hill beyond, taking a long look at the route over which Amanda had run.

"She's really alone out there, huh?" Georgie mused toward Dremmel as they padded back through the house to join Blake at the door he held open.

CHAPTER 18

Debbie Green had reached the top of the knoll in time to see Amanda slip into the woods on the other side, at the opening that marked the head of the trail Amanda had first explored with Rin and Ester, both now gone. Debbie Green paused at the top, her lungs gulping breaths as piercing fatigue spiked through her thighs. She started down the back side more slowly, trotting and rolling to a lumber by the time she reached the woodline below. She bent to peer into the opening. She did not bother to enter. She could never catch Amanda. She sat heavily upon the ground and leaned backward, propping her arms behind her. She gulped air and wondered what she should do. Maybe Amanda would come back on her own, Green thought. She would have to come back, the kennel keeper decided, because she had no other place to go.

"She's gotta come back," Green said aloud, as if she would convert the possibility to a certainty merely by shaping the words. "What can she do out here? There's nothing to do out here. She's gotta come back in an hour or two."

Feeling secure in the thought, she dismissed the concern and started back up the little hill, bent heavily forward and still desperately sucking for air. She made her way back slowly. She would sit in her work room and rest, she figured. She came around the compound and squared up toward the main entrance when unexpectedly she encountered Melinda Gates, who was walking to the door as well.

"Oh, you're out here," Melinda said. "I thought you'd be inside."

"I was inside before," Green stammered through her surprise. "Now I'm out here."

"Were you running?"

"Yeah. I was running just now."

"Don't you have any running clothes?"

"No. Yes. I mean, I wasn't *running* running. I mean, I wasn't running to get exercise. I just ran just now just to get back here."

"Back from where?" asked Melinda.

"What? Back from where? Oh, I was just outside. I just came out to go for a little walk. Then I thought I should run to get back."

"Well I'm glad I ran into you," said Melinda. "I'm just on my way over to start, you know, looking over the four guys – except I guess it's five guys now, isn't it? Now that ol' Gandhi is back. Reggie called me a little while ago to tell me he was back now."

"Right. Gandhi's back now."

"I figure it's not too late for me to give them all a quick look. I can spend a little bit of time with them now. I'll get to know each one. At least a little. I still have all the reports that you and Reggie did, too. I'll definitely read over all of those. There's still time for that too, right? I want to make sure I pick the right one. You know, the one with just the right personality. The right disposition. That's the one we'll pair up with little Amanda."

"Right," said Green between rapid breaths.

"Although, now, with Gandhi back, I don't know how necessary any of this is. Maybe we should have just stuck with him in the first place. But, well, they're all here now, and I guess I should give them all a shot. I cleared my calendar for this – to come down here and spend some time with them to evaluate them. I figure I'll spend fifteen minutes with each one, just to get to know them. I'll go over your reports, too, like I said. I'll do that later. Reggie told me that Amanda is just about ready to be mated, but I still have enough time to make the right selection for her husband, right? How is Amanda doing today, anyway?"

"Amanda? Well, she…"

While Green stammered, she and Melinda Gates reached the building entrance. They opened the door, started inside, but pulled up in startled surprise to see Dremmel, Georgie and Blake in the open work area, just crossing in a line from Amanda's quarters to re-enter their own. The three of them pulled up immediately too, struck and startled by the sudden entrance of the women. The two groups stayed suspended for a long instant, with Green and Gates agape at the sight of Dremmel, Georgie and Blake arrayed in a line and looking broadside back at the women with equal surprise and befuddlement.

Georgie moved first. The image of Amanda coiled in the lush, open forest had stayed foremost in his mind since Dremmel had showed George her escape route out back. Now, seeing the door propped open by the gaping Gates and Green as they stood suspended half inside the entrance, Georgie flung toward it on a wild impulse. He brushed instantly past the two women before they could react.

"Hey, where's he going!" Blake blurted. Unwilling to be outdone, he leaped immediately after Georgie. Blake writhed through the door and dashed with abandon at the heels of Georgie outside.

Only Dremmel stayed frozen.

"Don't let him get out," commanded Melinda Gates. She closed the door firmly before stepping into the work room to collar the still-frozen

Dremmel.

"Where does he go?" she shot back to Green, who stood at the entranceway still.

Green pointed to the door that opened into the quarters that Dremmel shared with Georgie, Blake and Web. Gates flung him inside.

Dremmel, shocked and stupefied, disoriented even as he stood inside his own familiar home, suddenly found himself staring nose-to-nose with Web, who had just come in from the yard to see if his housemates had returned.

"Hey, Dremmel, there you are," said Web. "I thought you said you'd be back right away. I was all alone over here. I got worried. I've been back and forth lookin' for you guys. I've been inside and outside about five times in the last two minutes."

Dremmel remained dumbstruck and disoriented.

"But listen to this," Web said. "Big Gandhi is outside. Did you know that? Just before I came in this last time just now I saw Big Gandhi come out."

Dremmel did not comprehend.

"Did you hear that, Dremmel?" Web said. "I was just outside. Big Gandhi's out there. I just said hi to him."

Still Dremmel remained silent.

"He's over at that other place, where Rin and Ester used to live. I said hi to him."

Dremmel stayed big eyed and mute.

"Come on out with me now," said Web. "I told him I'd go in and get you. You came back just in time. Let's hurry while he's still outside."

Web turned and trotted eagerly to the back entrance of their house. Dremmel followed him robotically. Web led him through the back door. But out in their yard, as Web raised his head to call a greeting across to Gandhi, he spied in the distance the racing figures of Georgie and Blake. Tucked low to the ground, Georgie sped with blurred strides toward the top of the knoll. Three steps behind him, Blake looked to lose a little distance each time their furious feet beat against the earth.

Gandhi saw them too. From across the fences he asked, "who are those two guys?"

"They look just like Georgie and Blake," said Web in reply.

"I met Blake when I was out here before," said Gandhi. "But who's Georgie?"

"He lives over here with us too," Web replied as he strained for comprehension. "He was just over at Amanda's. Dremmel and Blake went over there to let him out. Dremmel just got back. This is him right here. But Georgie and Blake aren't back yet. But . . .. Hey Dremmel," Web asked as he turned to his housemate, "Dremmel, where's Georgie and Blake?"

"That was them right there," said Dremmel still stunned but finally breaking his stupor.

"You mean now they got out too?"

"Now they got out too."

"That's right where Amanda ran, isn't it?" Web asked. "That's right where you showed me where Amanda ran. Are they going out after her? Are they going out now to bring Amanda back here?"

"I don't think so," said Dremmel.

"Wait a minute," Gandhi interrupted. "You mean Amanda who lives right here? You mean this Amanda, from right here? You mean she got out too?"

"Right," said Dremmel.

"When did she run off?"

"After we were out here before," Dremmel said flatly. "After she went inside and you went inside. Blake and I were still out here. A little while after you went inside we saw her run off over that hill over there."

"Debbie Green went to get her, right Dremmel?" asked Web. "That's what you told me before. You said Debbie Green already went to get her."

"Debbie Green's back now," droned Dremmel.

"So now those two are going out to get her?" Gandhi wondered.

"I don't think so," said Dremmel. "I think Georgie went after Amanda. Blake just went after Georgie."

"You mean Georgie went to get Amanda back?" Gandhi asked him.

"No, not exactly. It's more like he just went to get her."

"Hey, you don't mean... Who is this Georgie, anyway? Would he really do something like that to her?"

"I think so."

"Who is he?"

"He lives here with us. You haven't met him yet. Georgie's just crazy."

"I think you're all crazy," said Gandhi.

The three of them stood silently for a moment, gazing off over the rise where first Amanda and now Georgie and Blake had disappeared.

Gandhi said, "you're not going to just let him do that to her, are you?"

"There's nothing I can do about it," Dremmel answered.

"Yes there is," said Gandhi. "You can go out there and stop him."

"I can't stop him," said Dremmel. "How can I stop him? I can't get out there."

"I can," said Gandhi. He raised his head and scanned all along the top of the fence that surrounded his yard. He brought his gaze back to the far outside corner, where a right angle of chainlink pointed outward to the big world beyond the pen. "In that corner I bet I can grapple up out of here," he said.

"But you can't break out," Dremmel protested. "You just came back. You're supposed to stay here. You're supposed to stay here with us and we're all supposed to stay here together. Forever. Look at how nice this place is."

"It doesn't look so nice to me," said Gandhi. He trotted resolutely to the corner of his lot.

"You can't get over that," Web said to him. "The fence is too high. Blake jumps up on it all the time. He's the best jumper ever. But even Blake can't jump over it."

Gandhi paced back from the corner, reared low for power and bound mightily toward the wire-framed angle. He leaped high and clawed for holds in the open mesh of the fence, propelling himself high and still higher until he was able to curl over the top rail and, in one long, descending leap, drive himself down to the earth and outside to freedom.

Dremmel stared silently as Gandhi charged away, sprinting fast on the path of Amanda, Georgie and Blake. Web said, "You were right, Dremmel. He really is the best there can be."

CHAPTER 19

After Melinda Gates flung Dremmel into his quarters, she closed the door firmly and tried the handle with several hard jerks, pitting her full weight against the door to make sure it would not open. With the door latched fast, she turned back to Debbie Green, still speechless at the entrance where Georgie and Blake had escaped.

"What are they doing?" demanded Melinda. "Where in the hell are they going?"

"I have absolutely no idea," said Green.

"How did they get out of their pen?"

"I don't know."

"I can't believe this," fumed Gates. "With all that I'm doing for them – with all the I'm doing for all of their kind. How could they do this? How could they bolt out of here? Don't they have any gratitude for what I'm doing for them?"

"I don't know," Green said. Furtively she glanced around her work room. The area looked cluttered and disorderly, with its long countertop obscured beneath clutters and heaps and jumbles: cleaners in bottles, brushes, sponges, a pail, aerosol sprays, an old pizza box, two magazines, a sweatshirt rumpled in a mound with socks, a measuring cup, flashlight, fly swatter, foam cups with stained tops, dust pan, hand cream, pretzel bag, sun block and bug spray, z-fold towels, a spray hose, gum pack, plastic forks in a box with the top gouged open, one paper-wrapped straw, magnifying lens, wash pan, marker, and other stray bits of equipment, supplies and plain refuse she could have returned to shelves and cupboards or just tossed into the trash. She wished now that she had tidied the room the way Macklam had told her to do so many times.

"Where do you think they went?" Gates demanded from Green.

"I have no idea."

"Are they out there still? Can you see them through the window?"

"Not anymore. They ran off right away."

"But where could they be going?"

"I have no idea."

"Where's Macklam?" Melinda quizzed.

"He was out. I don't know where he is right now."

"Call him," Melinda ordered. "Call Reggie right away and have him go get them. He can get them the hell out of here, too. Maybe he should get them all out of here if that's the way they're going to behave, if that's how they're going to repay me. At least I have Amanda. And now Gandhi is back too. If not for those two I would cancel the whole project. At least with those two there's some hope. Forget about those four guys in there. Tell Reggie to get 'em out of here. I'm not going to waste my time with them. Let's go in and see Amanda. I need to calm my nerves for a while. Let's go in and visit Amanda for a while and I'll feel better about ever starting this whole thing."

Debbie Green stayed silent.

"Come on," said Melinda. "Let's go see Amanda. Which room is she in? Is she in this one?"

As Gates stepped toward the door next in line, Green said, "we can't go see Amanda right now."

"Why not? Is she out with Reggie again?"

"No."

"Then let's go see her."

"She's just out."

"What do you mean she's just out?"

"She's out. She's out there. Out there where those other two went."

"What? Out there? No she's not. That was just two of the guys who rushed out. Wasn't it? That wasn't Amanda. I know Amanda from when she's been around the office with Bill. She wasn't here just now. That was just two guys, right?"

"It was two guys just now. That was Georgie and Blake who ran out. But Amanda was already gone. Amanda ran out before you came."

"Before I came?"

"Before you came down just now to see them all. Just a little before that Amanda ran out when I opened her door. She went out the front door here and ran away in the same direction those two guys just went."

"Where was she going?"

"I have no idea."

"Didn't you try to stop her?"

"I ran after her as fast as I could. That's where I was when you met me coming back here just now. I was out chasing Amanda."

"Then where is she?"

"I couldn't catch her."

"Where did she go?"

"I don't know."

"Amanda ran off. I don't believe it. Has she even done this before?"

"No."

"Then why did she do it now?"

"I have no idea."

"Amanda ran off! I can't believe this. I can't breed dogs who aren't going to stay where they're supposed to stay. I don't think running off adds up to a good disposition, do you? Now I feel like I have to start all over again. Oh, this is taking just too much of my time. Ugh." She breathed hard for a moment. "At least now Gandhi is back. I should have just stuck with him in the first place. Who cares if Bill didn't like him. Let's go in and see Gandhi for a second. I need to know there's at least one good one left, at least one that's worth so much of my time."

"That's a great idea," said Debbie Green, instantly sparked by relief. "He's right in here. Right through this last door right here."

CHAPTER 20

When Melinda Gates told Reginald Macklam to cancel the breeding project, Macklam politely concealed his relief. He will close it down right away, he replied in a businesslike manner. But he needed to know what she wanted him to do with all the breeders. Melinda told him to sell off Georgie, Blake, Dremmel, Web, Gandhi and even Amanda. She told him to sell them all. Macklam politely explained that he would place each one in a suitable home. He skipped telling her that so far he had rounded up only Georgie, Blake and big Gandhi. Amanda was still missing. But Mrs. Gates didn't need to be bothered with all the small details, he figured. He will hunt more till he captures Amanda, Macklam reasoned. In the meantime, he thought, he will handle the shut-down without troubling Mrs. Gates about any of its niggling demands.

Right away Macklam moved Georgie, Blake, Dremmel, Web and Gandhi out of the kennel compound. He placed them in temporary holding until he could find each one a permanent home. He sent Gandhi back to the home he had just left. He let go of Debbie Green. He locked all the gates and the doors of the compound, figuring he would never have to enter again. Even though Amanda still was scurrying free in the woods, Macklam felt lightweight and liberated. So what if the breeding program had never come near to its goal. He suffered no guilt, remorse or regret for the failure. He had never signed on as a breeder. He had sidled accidentally into that role after beginning his first job here: to attach a dog to Bill Gates. In that he had succeeded. Or at least his part of the image program had succeeded. Rin had become Bill Gates' dog thoroughly and very convincingly, Macklam concluded. After that, the add-on assignment of Melinda's breeding had become a nagging hindrance for him. He didn't care that it failed. He felt eager to move on. Maybe he'll find another Hollywood assignment, he thought, one with hard and fast filming dates that will translate to deadlines and concrete goals that he will have to strive to achieve. He felt buoyed and eager, restless for the challenge. He anticipated the hubbub, the scrum, the accelerated effort and inescapable urgency that a deadline brings to a high-profile project like a big-budget film. This Gates job had brought him so little of that. Even the image-dog training had demanded too little. Despite the first failure with Gandhi, despite all the early objections thrown up by Bill Gates, the billionaire had taken to Rin rather quickly. The two had enmeshed so well that after a while Macklam had scarcely felt needed. He had felt like a highly paid kennel hand, simply delivering Rin according to the harried schedule set up by Bill Gates – hardly a role that Macklam had wanted. He had staved off boredom by getting away on so many excursions and long rambles with Rin and sometimes Amanda. He'll miss those, he thought.

He will miss Bill Gates too, he now realized as he prepared to enter the billionaire's office for what he took to be the last time. Gates had telephoned the trainer to set up the meeting. Maybe he wants to make sure all the keys are turned in, Macklam thought. Or maybe he just wants to say a final goodbye. Although Macklam didn't ordinarily succumb to bleary sentimentality, the thought brought him the pang of a final departure. As he settled into the room, he gazed wistfully around Gates' private work space. Macklam had never really liked the place. The clever coordination of all the suite's furnishings annoyed him. They amused him a little, too. The decorator had done the room so carefully that it looked like a showpiece. It wore the bland precision of a conception, a plan, an idea of what the office of the world's richest man *should* look like. Still, beneath all the glazing, Macklam picked up a primitive energy that he liked very much. It came from Gates himself, seated now at the big desk like a child outscaled on a bus seat.

Macklam did not mind the fact that Gates was not brilliant. On the contrary, he felt a close kinship with the billionaire because he recognized that Gates was really a lot like himself. Bill Gates was keen, perhaps, but at most it was a middling intelligence that did not seem to exceed his own. Still, it was enough, thought Macklam. He understood that, rather than brilliance, intensely competitive pride and unflagging determination could yield success as stunning as the business success enjoyed by Bill Gates. No doubt Gates had been helped along by some lucky turns of unpredictable circumstances. But Macklam couldn't hold the good fortune of the man against him. At root Bill Gates was just another guy who worked endlessly, driven by a contentious pride, a fractious will, and an unwillingness to fail. Similar qualities had pushed Macklam to a pinnacle in his own field. If his chosen profession as animal trainer did not yield the rewards available to a business executive like Billy Gates, well, that was just the way the world was ordered. Macklam felt content with his own life, so he didn't begrudge the higher stature and the greater wealth that Gates had obtained.

Besides, just a few days earlier – just before Melinda's big fracas with the breeding dogs and their sudden, subsequent banishment – Gates had asked Macklam to retrieve Rin for him. What a surprise that had been. Macklam had never, ever suspected that Gates would give even a passing thought to Rin after he had sent him away. But now Rin was here again, coiled comfortably beside Bill Gates in the billionaire's own inner sanctum. The sight gave Macklam one more reason to appreciate the businessman. While most every job that Macklam undertook ended successfully, this one was also ending well.

"He looks awfully contented right there," said Macklam with a feint toward Rin. "You wouldn't know he had ever been gone. You wouldn't think he'd ever been any place different."

"I forget he's here myself," said Gates. "Except that, well, I don't know. It's kind of hard to explain, but it's also like I never completely forget that he's here, either. It's almost like it's on a subconscious level or something. It's like . . . like …" He paused, searching to find the right phrasing.

"It's like somehow or other you're aware of another heartbeat. I know what you mean," said Macklam. "It's a lot like your own: you're never really aware of your own heartbeat, except that you are at some unconscious level. You'd certainly miss it if it left you," he chuckled.

"I know I'd miss mine," said Gates.

"But is that all it is then?" asked Macklam. "I've wondered, because when you called me to tell me you wanted Rin back, you never said why. I mean, we never really went into it that deeply. So ever since I went and got him for you, I've wondered what happened to change your mind."

"It goes back to that meeting we had a little while ago – the first time I told you to get rid of him. Remember? It gets back to what Cassie Welch said to me. She said he was no trouble at all. That part I agreed with. But she also said that he'd gotten to be a good friend. I think I just didn't realize it then. It's kind of like that heartbeat thing you just mentioned. It's just there and you really miss it if it's gone. It took his going away for me to realize how much I liked him around."

"It seems that you should have listened to Cassie back then. You would have saved us both a lot of bother," said Macklam.

"Yeah. Well, maybe. But that wasn't the only thing. The other thing that got me thinking was what Melinda said. Or, it was what she did, really. It was at that same meeting. It was when she decided to bring Gandhi back. He'd been gone for a while by then. But she just turned the whole thing around and told you to bring him back. She decided the whole thing in a split second like that and it got me thinking – after Rin here was gone and I realized I kind of missed having him around, it got me thinking, why not just change my mind and tell you to bring him back? Why not reverse it just like that, just like Melinda did? So I did."

"I'm awfully glad that you did," said Macklam. "As much as I like getting rid of all those others for your missus – I mean, I don't have anything against them, but I never really fancied myself running a breeding kennel. It just sort of happened here and I have to speak the truth and tell you that I feel awfully glad to shut it down and get rid of all those others. But as good as I feel about that, it made me feel a whole lot better to bring Rin back to you. As glad as I am about closing that kennel, I feel even gladder to see Rin right here with you now."

"Then how would you feel about bringing back another one?"

"What's that?"

"That's why I called you to come in for this meeting," said Gates. "I think there's one more thing I'd like to ask you to do for me."

"To bring back another?"

"It's for Melinda. But not for breeding or anything like that. It's just to have, the way I have Rin here. Because, when I heard that she shut down the kennel and sent them all away, I felt kind of bad for her. Not so much because the project had failed. Everybody could see that was coming a while ago. She just doesn't have the time. She already does too much. She probably never should have tried it in the first place. But she loves those Aussie dogs so much. That's why I felt bad for her: she doesn't have one anymore. So I figured, why not get one? She can just have one for herself, like I have Rin here. She doesn't have to turn it into some grandiose project like that breeding thing was. That was too much. It was too complicated. But she can still just have a friend around, right?"

"That's right," said Macklam. "Of course she can. I agree with you one-hundred percent."

"So, what about one of the ones we already had around here? How many of them were there? Six? Seven?"

"We had six after Gandhi came back," replied Macklam.

"That should be enough to choose from," said Gates.

"That's more than enough," answered Macklam.

"The thing I don't know is, which one," Gates went on. "I barely even saw any of those others. That's what I need you for, Reggie. I need to know, who's the best one to bring back for Melinda?"

"That's really not too hard," said Macklam. "To me it's as clear as can be that the one she'll want is Amanda. She's intelligent, loyal – she has just the right disposition that your wife was looking for in the first place. It's definitely Amanda. Although, I have to say, Gandhi would do very nicely too. But with Rin here, since they're going to be together, I think Amanda is the far better choice."

"Amanda is the one you used to bring around here sometimes, isn't she?" asked Gates. "Isn't she the one who used to stay here real calmly with Rin when you brought her around?"

"That's Amanda," Macklam answered. "She was perfect here with Rin. She's the perfect one to keep for your missus because she'll be the perfect companion for Rin right here. We have to remember that, whichever one we choose for your wife, we're also choosing as a partner for Rin."

"Then Amanda it is," summed Gates. "I take it you can bring her back right away. I mean, you shipped them all away just a day or so ago. Right?

They've barely been gone at all. Right?"

"Well, that's correct," explained Macklam. "But Amanda is going to be a little more of a problem. You see, I haven't been able to get Amanda back yet. She's still out there in the forest some place. She was one of the four that ran off. She was the first one, in fact. I brought in the other three. Brought them in right away, in fact. But Amanda's been elusive. She's trying awfully hard not to get caught. That can make it tough."

"Then how come you got the others so easily?"

"Because the others didn't want to stay out there. The others weren't trying to evade me. Especially the first two I caught. The first two were Blake and Georgie. I found them almost right away, but that's because they wanted to be found. They were awfully beat up. They needed my help pretty badly. I don't know who got 'em, but someone sure gave them an awfully good thrashing. When I found 'em they were limping and punctured and cut. They were aching to be found. I think they just wanted to get out of the woods and get themselves patched up.

"But, now, I have to say that with Gandhi it was different," Macklam went on. "I got him later, because he wasn't so eager to be found. He wasn't beat up at all. He was with Amanda, and she wasn't beat up either. Neither one of them looked like they had a scratch on them. Gandhi wasn't so easy to corral but I think he kind of gave himself up as a decoy. It sounds kind of crazy, I know. But at the time I had the distinct impression that I got Gandhi because he was giving Amanda time to get away – like he was giving himself up to me so that I wouldn't get her, so that she would be able to get away while I was tied up with him. And she did. She dashed away a lot faster than I ever thought she could move. I haven't seen her since. I've been out a few times since then and I still haven't seen her."

"Do you think you will?" queried Gates. "If Amanda is the best choice for Melinda, then you have to get her back."

"Oh, I'll get her back," Macklam said. "At least I fully intend to. It's just that so far it's been a lot more difficult than I ever expected."

"How are you going to do it?" asked Gates.

"I don't know yet," said Macklam. "I think maybe it's time to change strategies. In fact..." He paused as he looked thoughtfully at Rin, who himself watched attentively as the conversation progressed. "In fact," Macklam said, "if you'd be willing to part with Rin here for just a few hours, I think he might be just the strategy I need. I think maybe Rin can track her down and find her. He knows those woods out there as well as I do. In fact, I'm sure he knows them better. We used to walk out there quite a bit. We used to walk out there with Amanda. I bet you he'll know where to find her. I'm certain he'll know where to look. He knows all the trails and all the old logging roads out there better than anyone else."

Rin sprang immediately into the task. The instant Macklam set him loose around the back of the just-closed kennel, Rin sprinted up and over the knoll, running faster than Macklam had ever witnessed him run before. Macklam himself dashed resolutely up the slope, striding rapidly against the incline and reaching the top more readily than Debbie Green had reached it a few days before. Even so, Rin had already disappeared into the treeline below by the time Macklam could see down the back side of the hillock. With Rin already out of sight, Macklam hustled down toward the trail entrance at a more moderate pace. He couldn't possibly keep up with him anyway. He didn't need to, because Rin knew exactly where to go without any guidance. Macklam strode into the forest feeling secure that, by the time he encountered him again, Rin would be walking with Amanda.

Inside the forest Rin did not ease back on his furious pace. Outstretched and striving, he continued to charge at full tilt even though the ground amid the trees here was mounded and broken and cut. He leaped across obstructing stones and he bound above the gnarled surface roots of trees that grew anchored on the path. He veered and darted around quick-turns that avoided the statuesque trunks. He marveled at his speed. He marveled at how he kept the frantic pace. His strength did not wane. The distance did not overtake him. He felt joy. The exhilaration stoked his zeal, so that Rin's excitement fed itself, with excitement for his unrestrained movement egging him to run all the faster and faster. He streaked so rapidly through the occluded wood that he might have missed Amanda altogether, except that he recognized that some insight, hunch, sensation or intuition would stop him wherever she waited. He sprinted the full distance of the path that delivered him to the defunct rail cut running level through the woods. Without a pause he turned and he dashed, running furiously still, up the straight trail, running inside an off-roader wheel rut to miss all obstructions and increase his speed by pounding on the packed and level dirt. With vigor and resolve he raced all the way to the overgrown, obscured siding where the rail line once had split to service a village. He cut onto the side-shoot and torpedoed through the dense brush that grew riotously now where once the earth had been cleared. Rin shot blindly through the concealing scrub until suddenly he emerged in the open expanse where the village once had stood. He pulled up abruptly and, standing, he shouted, "Amanda. Amanda. Amanda. Are you here?"

She stepped out of concealment, shuddering first, made timid by her surprise.

"Rin?" she spoke.

"It's me," he panted jubilantly.

She dashed to him.

"I knew you'd come here," she said as she nuzzled him and she embraced him. "I knew this was the perfect place to wait for you. I knew you'd be here."

"It's the first place I came," he said.

"It's the perfect place for us to stay. The two of us here together. We can live here and no one will bother us. I found some places where it's okay to stay. They're sheltered and we'll stay warm and we'll stay out of the rain and the cold."

"But now we don't have to," he said. "Not anymore. They want you to come back there. That's what I ran here all the way to tell you. You can come back now and we'll be together."

"But we can be together here," she responded. "I already found some places with some cover for over our heads. I cleaned them up already. They're already ready for us to stay. I did it while I was waiting for you."

"But we don't have to stay here," Rin repeated. "They want you to come back now. *I* want you to come back. We can be together there."

"But those others are there," Amanda protested. "I don't want to stay there with those others around. I want to stay here where I'll be just with you."

"But the other's aren't there anymore," said Rin. "They're all gone now."

"They are?"

"Yes, they are. They're gone now. They all disappeared."

"They did?"

"Yes, they're gone."

"Where did they go?"

"I don't know where they went. I don't care. They just vanished. Now it's just me there. And now it's you, too. It's just the two of us together. We'll be there together now and it will be the best place there could ever be."

ABOUT THE AUTHOR

Jeffrey Zygmont writes stories about free people who possess rebellious impulses. His books tell about independent characters in conflict with collected groups and their constraining beliefs. In addition to **I Am Bill Gates' Dog**, that theme of defiant independence animates two other current novels: **Adman in the Games of 2046,** and **The Dropout**.

Jeffrey Zygmont's short fiction has appeared in the anthology **The Literature of Work**, and in periodicals ranging from *New Hampshire Journal* to the magazine *Twin Cities Business Monthly*. His poetry has appeared in the journal *Not Just Air*. Two of his poems received nominations for the annual Pushcart Prize, a respected literary award. They are *Wife Poem XXVII*, nominated in 2008, and *Menopause*, nominated in 2009. Zygmont's novel **The Dropout** was the July 2002 Featured Selection of the pioneering web publisher Online Originals.

As a journalist, Zygmont has published articles in magazines and newspapers including *Boston Magazine, Boston Woman, Business Week, CFO Magazine, The Christian Science Monitor, Cigar Aficionado, Gannett Newspapers, Inc Magazine, The Boston Globe Sunday Magazine*, and *Robb Report*. He was the automobile columnist for *Omni Magazine*, a technology columnist for *PC Computing Magazine*, and an editor for *High Technology Magazine*. His non-fiction books are **Microchip; An Idea, Its Genesis and the Revolution It Created**, and **The VC Way; Investment Secrets from the Wizards of Venture Capital**, which was translated into Chinese for sale in that country.